Hildur, Queen (

Hildur, Queen of the Elves
and Other Icelandic Legends

retold by J. M. Bedell
introduced and translated by Terry Gunnell

Interlink Books

An imprint of Interlink Publishing Group, Inc.
Northampton, Massachusetts

This edition first published in 2016 by

INTERLINK BOOKS
An imprint of Interlink Publishing Group, Inc.
46 Crosby Street, Northampton, Massachusetts 01060
www.interlinkbooks.com

Library of Congress Cataloging-in-Publication Data
Bedell, J. M. (Jane M.)
  Hildur, queen of the elves : and other Icelandic legends / by J. M. Bedell;
introduction and new translations by Terry Gunnell.
    p. cm.
  Includes bibliographical references.
  ISBN 1-56656-633-9 (pbk.)
  ISBN 13: 978-1-56656-633-9
  1. Folklore—Iceland. I. Title.
  GR215.B43 2005
  398.2'094912—dc22
                          2005013185

Printed and bound in the United States of America

To request our complete 40-page full-color catalog,
please call us toll free at **1-800-238-LINK,** visit our
website at **www.interlinkbooks.com**, or write to
Interlink Publishing
46 Crosby Street, Northampton, MA 01060
e-mail: info@interlinkbooks.com

"*[Folktales are] the offspring of fancy and popular poetry, never dying out so long as the flame of imagination is not extinct in the minds of the people.*"

—Gudbrandur Vigfússon, preface to *Icelandic Legends*, collected by Jón Árnason

Contents

*A new translation by Terry Gunnell

Acknowledgments

The tales in this book are not direct translations from original manuscripts. In an attempt to engage my readers, I kept most of the marvelous details translated in the cited texts (most often Jón Árnason, from the 1954–1961 version of his seminal *Íslenskar þjóðsögur og ævintýri*: Icelandic Folktales and Fairy Tales), but retained the right to use all the techniques available to any storyteller of fiction—writing scenes, creating suspense and drama, and varying points of view. Any inaccuracies in this book rest with me, not with the cited translators or Terry Gunnell.

I hope readers will enjoy the drama of these stories, knowing that they evolved through the centuries in the most beautiful but harshest of lands. The early Icelandic people willingly endured the island's climate and terrain but found strength, comfort, and distraction in sharing these stories around an evening fire. I also hope that you sense the playful spirit of the Icelandic people and their boundless enthusiasm for defining the indefinable aspects of human existence. The heart and soul of Iceland can be felt in the rich context of every line of each story.

A special thanks to Llanerch Press in Ceredigion, the current publishers of Árnason's *Icelandic Legends*, translated by George E. J. Powell and Eiríkur Magnússon; Tempus Publishing, the current publishers of *Icelandic Folktales and Legends* by

Jacqueline Simpson; and Iceland Review, the current publishers of *Ghosts, Witchcraft and the Other World* (Icelandic Folktales I) and *Elves, Trolls and Elemental Beings* (Icelandic Folktales II), translated by Alan Boucher. And to Jacqueline Simpson for her personal interest in this project.

Introduction
by Terry Gunnell

Readers of these stories should try to envisage the context in which they were usually told. Texts are one thing, but oral accounts are always strongly colored by the setting in which they are heard, and by the style and character of the people who tell them. In the case of the Icelandic legends, one can expect most of these stories to have been told during dark winter evenings, in the relatively cramped and stuffy confines of an Icelandic *baðstofa*. This was the room in which most people living on Icelandic farms from the Middle Ages until the early 20th century would have both slept and worked when not engaged in arduous farm work or fishing for the farmer that owned both the farm they lived in and the land surrounding it.

The *baðstofa*, which might have been about six meters by two, had thick walls made of turf and few windows to let in light. It would usually have had two rows of small beds running along either side of the room, each covered in rough woolen blankets. During waking hours these would have served as seats when people ate their meals or did indoor chores. The beds themselves would have been filled with hay, moss, or even seaweed. Commonly, each bed would have been slept in by two people who might sleep in opposite directions (head to feet) in order to make better use of the space. While the farmer and his wife might have a separate room, the farmer's children would usually have slept in the *baðstofa* with other relations, visitors, and any farm workers who had been employed for the year. The *baðstofa* itself was commonly situated at the end of a long, dark, and narrow corridor leading back from the front of the farmhouse. This too would have been largely built of turf, just like the rest of the farmhouse, and would have been hung with various farming implements. Running off either side of this corridor were other rooms—storerooms, a reception room, a pantry, and a smoke-filled kitchen. This kitchen would have been equipped with a large, eternally burning open fire, which provided much of the main heat for the farmhouse. In the roof above the fire, one might have found smoked meat or fish hanging, their odors adding to the general complex flavor of the Icelandic homestead.

On the surface, obvious comparisons can be made to the hobbit houses envisioned by J. R. R. Tolkien (himself a great Icelandophile). But comfort and coziness were not words that would immediately spring to the minds of the inhabitants of an Icelandic farmhouse. Such words were certainly rarely used by the English and German aristocratic travellers who visited the wilds of Iceland during the eighteenth and nineteenth centuries. As Sabine Baring Gould wrote of one such house in 1862:

> Looking at the front of the house, one observes five or more gables made of wood, painted red or black, wedged between turf walls from four to ten feet thick. The apex of the gable is seldom above twelve feet from the ground, very generally only eight, and is adorned with wooden horns, or weathercocks. Under the central gable is the door, around which are crooks upon which the stockings

of the family are hung to dry on windy and sunny days. Passing through the door, one enters a long dark passage, too low for a person to stand upright in it, leading to a ladder which gives access to the bathstófa (sic), or common eating, working, and sleeping apartment. This room is lighted by two or more glass panes, three inches square, inserted in the roof and sealed in so as to never be opened for the admission of pure air. The walls are lined with beds, and the end is divided off by a wooden mock-partition (never closed by a door) so as to form a compartment: here the father and mother of the family sleep, together with such visitors as cannot be accommodated in the guest chamber. In the bathstófa sleep all the people connected with the farm, two or even four in a bed, with the head of one at the feet of the other. The beds are lockers in the wall, lined with wood, and with wooden partitions between them. They are arranged along the room much like berths in a cabin, or the cubilia in a catacomb. Each is supplied with a mattress, feather bed or quilt, and home-woven counterpane. The Icelanders not only sleep in this room, but eat in it, making sofas of the beds, and tables of their knees. In it is spent the long dark winter, with no fire, and each inmate kept warm by animal heat alone. The stifling foulness of the atmosphere can hardly be conceived, and, indeed, is quite unendurable to English lungs (Boucher 111–112).

When the climate started rapidly declining after the 13th century, the Icelanders moved from the front rooms of their farmhouses back into these baðstofur (pl.), which were furthest from the front door and therefore warmest. (Literally, this word means the "bathroom," but not indoor baths in our sense of the word, even if hot springs did make hot water relatively easy to come by in some places. Instead, it was closer to a sauna, originally warmed by a fire in one corner.)

Until the 19th century, many people on this northerly island found themselves forced to scrape a meagrely existence off what was left available to them on the land, battered as they were by winds and snow in wintertime, and also by a succession of natural disasters and plagues. These ranged from a form of the Black Death that struck in the early 15th century, to pack ice, earthquakes, and volcanic eruptions, which reached a peak at the time of the Laki eruptions of 1783–1784. During this final catastrophe, more than two-thirds of the livestock and 9,000 people (about a fifth of the population) met their deaths. In some perhaps slightly romantic senses, the atmosphere of the *baðstofa* in midwinter during this period might be compared to that of the underground stations of London during the Blitz in World War II. Outside in the darkness there were numerous perils and threats (echoed and personified by the folk beliefs of the time). Inside, in the crowded and smoky *baðstofa*, lit only by a few small windows (often covered by a dried animal membrane rather than glass) and extremely smoky shark, cod, or seal oil lamps, a strong sense of community prevailed.

It is commonly argued that Iceland was a classless society, but the legends told in the Icelandic *baðstofur* belie this. The fact is, a large percentage of the people were workers. Many had no land of their own. Those not struggling to survive as tenants were taken on annually to live and work with the farmers who owned the land. As farm workers they had few real rights and little job security. The men, in addition to working the farm, would often be sent long distances across the country in the depth of winter to stay and work on the tiny rock- and turf-built fishing stations of the southern and western coasts. Here, during the short hours of daylight, they would spend several months fishing the icy and often turbulent North Atlantic in large open rowing boats. The wives and children who saw these men off could never be sure if they would see them again the following spring. In such circumstances, superstition was rife.

In a class above the landowning farmers were the churchmen. Alongside them were the state officials, many of whom were Danish in these colonial times, and the merchants, who were also largely Danish as a result of the restrictive Danish trade monopoly that was in force during the 19th century. Nonetheless, within the *baðstofa* as the stories were told and people of all classes sat and worked together, these boundaries might momentarily disappear. During the evening storytelling sessions, people were simply people, and everyone liked a good, well-told story.

Such evening gatherings, known as *kvöldvökur* (pl. literally, "evening wakes"), were a phenomenon well known in most Scandinavian rural communities from the earliest of times. In many ways they go back to the communal entertainments of the Viking hall, which had housed a similar community to that of the *baðstofa*, albeit on a somewhat larger scale. Like the Irish and Scottish *ceilidh* gatherings, the *kvöldvaka* was a form of self-made winter evening entertainment involving story, music, and song. Stories, of course, would have been told at any communal gathering in Iceland, whether in the fields or in the cowshed. The *kvöldvaka*, however, was the archetypal setting. Here, as the members of the household sat around the *baðstofa* doing their winter evening chores (teasing, carding, spinning, or knitting wool—tasks done by both sexes; sewing shoes or shoe linings; carving or whittling wood; entwining ropes and string; repairing small farm implements or clothes), they passed the time by encouraging one man or woman to stand or sit at the head of the room and temporarily transport them to another world. The storyteller would recite, read, or retell passages from the Bible or the ancient sagas, chant *rímur* (a special form of Icelandic ballad), or simply read or tell folktales, most of which, prior to the appearance of the first collections from the mid-19th century, would have been passed on as oral tradition.

The storytellers themselves would commonly have been people living and working on the farm. They were men or women known for their memories or storytelling abilities, people who knew how to build up an atmosphere and play with character, raconteurs who had a talent for humor or the creation of suspense. At other times, they might have been overnight visitors: vagrants who frequently wandered between farmsteads, entertaining their hosts as they went; skilled workers who had particular abilities or travellers with imported wares to sell; or sheriffs, bishops, priests and other lofty officials who needed a roof over their heads as they traversed the country on official business. Such travelling people as these were the real bearers of rumor, news, and legend between farms in different areas. At the same time, their arrival would have inspired the repetition and embellishment of old well-known local tales.

The collections of Icelandic legends that have been made over the centuries underline the fact that in Iceland's past, the landscape itself represented a kind of storybook for its inhabitants. Every farm; every valley; every river, waterfall, and stream; every mountain, rock, or cliff had seen numerous generations come and go. Each, indirectly, had a tale to tell. In that sense, the land connected the people directly with their ancestors who had shaped the environment; it drew them to recall tales of the "huge-boned" settlers of Viking times, of notable great men landing fishing boats in impossible conditions, and of outlaws and officials who survived desperate journeys through storms and swollen rivers. Icelandic legends reflect a common belief that the settlers of the country were near giants, much greater people than those of the present. However, the stories of the land also drew the listeners to consider the powers and forces that lived just out of immediate view within these same rocks, streams, waves, and waterfalls, and behind the mists and sand clouds of the desert.

Legends—as opposed to wondertales, or fairy tales—always tend to be more closely related to particular places, times, and people. They are presented as truth rather than fiction, even though that truth may often stretch the imagination to the breaking point. Within this group of legends, however, there is some variety. To start with, there are "experience legends," or memorats, which we tell about unusual or newsworthy events that have occurred to us personally. Once these tales have been heard, retold, and passed on by others, however, they start transforming into more traditional legends that might become widely known within a particular area. They take on customary shape, gain prologues, build-ups, strong adjectives, and moments of exaggeration. At that point they might even start blending or becoming confused with other more widely-known traditional tales that have travelled still further, and are known throughout different countries. Such legends, usually referred to as migratory legends, have a habit of putting down new roots in places where the environment is fertile and fitting, especially when they end up in the hands of an expert storyteller. Typical examples of such locally adapted foreign legends in Iceland are tales such as those of the seal-folk, the waterhorse, and the changeling. The appearance of such legends underlines the fact that, in spite of its centuries of hardship, Iceland was far from being culturally isolated.

In this context, it should be remembered that from the beginning, Iceland was settled by people who came from a wide expanse of territory and a near endless variety of different cultures. Many came from pagan Scandinavia. Others, especially slaves and concubines, came from Christian Ireland and Scotland. A number were northern Sami. Even among the western and southern Scandinavians who came to Iceland at the time of settlement in the late 9th century, there would have been a multiplicity of beliefs and local traditions, something immediately seen even today by anyone who takes a cursory peek at the various collections of mainland Scandinavian folk legends. In this sense, Iceland was one of the first multicultural societies to be established in Europe.

The settlers of Iceland, however, all believed in a world that was populated by local spirits. They seem to have believed that the land itself was under the "ownership" (or protection) of these potentially dangerous spirits. They also felt it necessary to pacify these spirits with regular offerings of food and drink, or at least to attempt to live in harmony with them. Such ideas are seen especially clearly in those early

Icelandic accounts that tell how people who wished to settle a new area of land first had to bring "civilization" symbolically to it by circling it with fire and thereby also "cleaning" it. One early medieval law stipulates that anyone planning to come to Iceland by sea had to remove the animal figureheads from their ships in order to avoid frightening the nature spirits away. Clearly, these spirits had some use.

Such beliefs continue even into our own time, in one way or another. They are typified by those ideas concerning the *jólasveinar* (Christmas Lads) and the legend of Grýla loved by all Icelandic children. As in the past, these figures are still supposed to inhabit the local mountains of each township, and as Christmas approaches, they are said to come down into the settlements one by one, leaving small offerings in children's shoes as they arrive. After Christmas, they gradually return to the place of their origin. In a sense, the *jólasveinar* represent the approaching darkness and winter at this low ebb in the Icelandic year. They and their supernatural kindred are the ones who really "control" the landscape. The Icelandic people understand themselves to be little more than tenants with little control over their environment—something about which glaciers, volcanoes, and earthquakes constantly serve as reminder.

The nature spirits that appear in this book closely reflect this worldview and wariness toward nature. These figures are intimately related to the landscape, but their personal characteristics and names also serve to underline Iceland's early cultural connections and the origins of the settlers in both the Scandinavian and the Celtic worlds. The most commonly known figures in this sense are the *álfar* (elves) or *huldufólk* (hidden people), the names of which are now (and in earlier legends) generally interchangeable. The word *álfar* occurs in Old Icelandic texts, but refers to more godlike beings than those talked about today. The word *huldufólk* is closely related to the Norwegian *huldre*, which is used for similar beings. Both words must come from a shared root and shared way of thinking, and there can be little doubt that these figures have their main roots in early Scandinavian folk belief. Nonetheless, several interesting features of the *huldufólk* also suggest that they also have been strongly influenced by Scottish or Irish views concerning the "fairy folk."

In general terms, the *huldufólk*, like the Irish fairies, are seen as inhabiting the landscape, especially the rocks and cliffs around settlements. Unlike many of the Scandinavian elf figures, they rarely live in the earth beneath farms. Furthermore, as with the Irish fairies, there are faint suggestions that the *huldufólk* may have once been associated with dead ancestors. One or two of the Icelandic sagas set in western Iceland, an area that initially had quite close Gaelic connections, suggest that the dead were believed to inhabit certain rocks and mountains. Iceland, like mainland Scandinavia, also shares with the Gaelic-speaking peoples several common legends and beliefs about the necessity of effective cooperation taking place between the elfin folk and human beings. The most well known is that of the Midwife to the Fairies (Migratory Legend, or ML, 5070 in the system developed by Norwegian folklorist Reidar Christiansen), where a human is requested to help a fairy or elf-woman give birth (see "The Elf-woman in Childbirth").

Much like the Norwegian *huldre/underjordisk* (hidden or underground people), the Icelandic *huldufólk* represent a mixture of the early *álfar* (elves) and *nátturuvættir* (nature spirits) mentioned in the Icelandic sagas and ancient Eddic poems. The former appear to have been semi-godlike (reminiscent of figures like Titania or Oberon and Tolkien's elves), while the latter, as their name suggests, were simple, but no less necessary spirits of the landscape. In the Icelandic legends first recorded in the eighteenth and nineteenth centuries, the *huldufólk* seem on the other hand to have been near mirror-images of those humans who told stories about them—except that they were usually beautiful, powerful, alluring, and free from care, while the Icelanders were often starving and struggling for existence. The *huldufólk* seem in many ways to represent the Icelander's dreams of a more perfect and happy existence. As such, these folk were a dangerous temptation for a godfearing people who were supposed to be satisfied with their lot on earth, steadfastly awaiting the joys of the world to come rather than expecting too much of the present.

The legends depict the *huldufólk* as living in communities, having farms, going fishing, moving house, having children, falling in love, getting married, and dying just like human beings. Furthermore, in Icelandic legends, in slight contrast to many mainland Scandinavian beliefs, they often have churches, priests, and legal officials (see, for example, "The Elf-Steeple"). And unlike many of their Norwegian relations—such as those reflected in Ibsen's *Peer Gynt*—the Icelandic *huldufólk* have no obvious bestial features. They do not have animal tails or animal snouts. Indeed, it is often difficult to tell the difference between them and normal human beings. The same applies to their superior breeds of livestock, which easily manage to blend in with those owned by humans. The close connections between the *huldufólk* and human beings are regularly stressed in the legends. We hear of love affairs taking place between them (see "The Girl at the Shieling" and "Katla's Dream") and also their desire to steal human children, replacing them with unwanted, senile men. The same idea is seen in those legends, also well known in Scandinavia, telling of the *huldufólk* as the lost "other" children of Adam and Eve or Adam's forgotten former wife Lilith, who was supposedly dumped because of her "unreasonable" demands for equality. However related the *huldufólk* might be to human beings, they most certainly inhabit the same landscape, and as with any neighbors, there is need for cooperation. As the legends demonstrate, such cooperation (generally following the conditions set by the *huldufólk*) can bring great reward, as when the supernatural beings express their gratitude by sharing the benefits of their greater wealth and knowledge of the future. Failure to cooperate or help, however, can bring about tragedy.

Many older Icelanders still believe in the existence of spirits that live within the countryside. A majority of other Icelanders, even if they do not directly "believe," would be wary of denying the possibility that the *huldufólk* might exist. Hence the numerous examples that can be found today in 21st-century Iceland of roads being built around sites (usually large rocks) where the *huldufólk* are believed to live. There is, however, one interesting difference between the modern beliefs concerning these spirits and those known in the past, in that today's *huldufólk* are still commonly seen as living like late 19th-century Icelandic farmers. In the common view today, they live in turf houses, ride horses, and wear 19th-century national dress. This change is a natural result of the first main collections of Icelandic legends having appeared in print in the late 19th century, thereby underlining in black and white for posterity what the *huldufólk* were supposed to look like. In modern beliefs and legends, they have thus come to represent the old rural world, with its values and close connections to nature, as opposed to a mechanized world of technological advances. Had the legends never been published, perhaps the *huldufólk* would have attained cell phones, cars, and Internet connections by now.

The *huldufólk*, however, were not the only spirits to inhabit the Icelandic rural landscape. In the days before the arrival of electric light, Iceland, with its low midwinter sun that briefly rolls across the horizon, its jagged human-like silhouettes of lava that seem to move as you blink, its rising clouds of hot steam, its juddering, grinding earthquakes, its spluttering mud pools, and its occasional whirling figures of dust, sand, or snow that appear and disappear in a moment, has always been highly conducive to beliefs about the existence of supernatural figures. Hence the numerous tales of trolls, which in Iceland have less of the spike-haired punk about them than those one might spy in a modern Norwegian souvenir store. Icelandic trolls, like those originally known in Scandinavia, are really the degraded relations of the earlier *jötnar* or "ice giants" that competed as equals with the gods in Old Nordic mythology. Less attractive, less wise, and less numerous than their forebears, they are nonetheless still credited as having had a large role to play in shaping the landscape, albeit by regularly turning to stone whenever they are tricked into staying around after sunrise. In the later Icelandic legends, they seem on their way to becoming an endangered species. Like the original Grýla (in the legend of the same name), they tend to live alone and are well aware that their time is nearly up. Spiritually, they have not moved past pagan times: as a number of legends from both mainland Scandinavia and Iceland show, the trolls are decidedly non-Christian, having little tolerance for church bells, hymns, or churchmen (except as a form of sushi).

Alongside the land-based supernatural figures noted above, there are a number of others more directly connected to water. Most of these, once again, find close relations in both Scandinavian and Gaelic folk belief and legend. Among them are the *nykur* or water horse (cf. the Scottish kelpie), which inhabits freshwater lakes and poses a particular threat to children; the water monsters that inhabit certain lakes like Lagarfljót in the east of Iceland; the wise *marbendill* or *marmennill* (merman) who lives in a farm beneath the surface of the sea and can—if well treated—provide knowledge of the future; the water cattle with the unique air bladders placed beneath their noses that allow them to breath underwater; and the seal-folk who shed their seal skins and dance naked on seashores on New Year's Eve, the most powerful time of the year for Iceland's supernatural spirits. (It is then that Icelandic elves are said to move their homes, if they wish.) Noticeably, as in Norway, there are few mermaids to be seen.

The legends also tell of a number of other monstrous figures that are quite unique to Iceland. These include the *fjörulalli*, an animal-like creature that rises from the rocks on a beach at night to chase unwitting passers-by; the *skoffín*, the result of a male fox's mating with a female cat; the *skuggabaldur*, the offspring of a male cat and a female fox or dog; and the *urðarköttur*, another powerful and ferocious cat-like creature that comes into being after a cat has lain on a corpse in a graveyard for three winters. The latter three, along with Grýla's man-eating Christmas Cat, seem to underline a deep-rooted wariness that the Icelanders of the past seem to have had for feline creatures.

These Icelanders did not only believe themselves to be surrounded by other supernatural races and creatures—they also saw themselves as constantly under threat from certain members of their own kind, especially outlaws, certain evil magicians, and the not-so-dearly departed. Outlaw legends were at one time a very popular genre of Icelandic folktale and in many ways are the "human" equivalent of tales of people being kidnapped by trolls or *huldufólk*. Many of the outlaw legends verge on being fairy tales in structure if not in length. Like the trolls and the *huldufólk*, the Icelandic outlaws were believed to inhabit the wild. They are sometimes depicted as living in rich, hidden communities in lost fertile valleys accidentally stumbled upon by lonely travellers who get lost in a fog, a common motif in outlaw tales and also in Gaelic fairy legends.

Reading between the lines, we can see the Icelanders' dream of a better, more perfect world existing just out of reach. Legends like these also seem to imply a belief that the wilderness was full of powerful outlaw figures like the famous Eyvindur of the Mountains. They have roots in the Icelandic sagas, which were also read out loud in the *kvöldvökur*. These works involve a number of memorable heroic Robin Hood-like outlaw heroes, such as Gísli Súrsson in *Gísla*

saga, and Grettir Ásmundarson in Grettis saga—
though without the bit about stealing from the rich and
giving to the poor. The Icelanders seemed to be
thinking primarily of their own survival. The legends,
with their constantly repeated captures, enslavements,
and escapes, can be compared to the basic storylines of
archetypal Indian movies of the 1960s and 1970s like
Soldier Blue, *Little Big Man*, and *A Man Called Horse*.
They provide interesting insight into the values and
hardships of Icelandic life in the past, especially the
attitudes toward authority and to the poverty suffered
by so many. Occasionally, the outlaw is depicted as a
troll-like monster, a form of Hannibal Lecter, a constant
threat to anyone who crosses the wilderness. At other
times, he is shown as someone for whom the storyteller
has great sympathy: a person who has broken the law
either out of great need, injustice, or by apparent
accident, as in those legends that tell of brothers and
sisters running away into the mountains after
committing incest, a crime that could be punished with
death. The interest in these tales, however, waned as
Iceland began to be mapped in ever greater detail and a
more realistic knowledge of the wilderness ensued. An
improved system of justice also came into being. By the
end of the 19th century, the outlaw legend seems to have
faded in popularity, along with the troll legend and the
fairy tale. One finds far fewer legends of this type in
more recent collections of folktales.

Those legends concerning magicians, on the other
hand, seem to have lived on. Even today, the
University of Iceland has a statue of a magician as one
of its most popular visual motifs in booklets and other
forms of advertisment. As with the tales of trolls,
huldufólk, and outlaws, stories about magicians go

back a long way in Icelandic culture. They have their roots in myths about the god Óðinn and in sagas telling of various kinds of rune magic, magical protection, the casting of illusions, and manipulation of the weather. In earlier saga accounts, the implication was that both women and men were involved in magical activities. But in the later legends, as in the Icelandic witch-trials from the western fjords in the 17th century, men were most often the workers of magic. Unlike its neighboring countries, Iceland has very few witch figures in its legends, largely because in Icelandic society, women rarely lived alone. As has been noted, few people owned land, and those who did rarely tried to work a farm alone. In the rare case that a woman found herself alone, she would usually have been taken to live on the farm of a relation. Those few witch legends that exist largely involve the sending of a familiar (in Iceland a being known as a *tilbera* made of wool, a bone, and blood) to steal milk from cows—a traditional story in both the Scandinavian and Gaelic countries. There are a few witch-ride legends like those found in Scandinavia and elsewhere in Europe, but in Iceland the women in question rarely fly to meet Satan at a Black Sabbath. On the contrary, they are usually "caught" flying to visit friends or their parents.

There are a number of other interesting features about the Icelandic magicians that are worth noting. First of all, most of these figures are priests, and like their fellow magical men of God in mainland Scandinavia, most are Lutheran ministers from the 16th, 17th, and 18th centuries. The most famous Icelandic magician, Sæmundur the Wise, is an exception in that he comes from the early Middle Ages. Secondly, the storytellers' sympathies usually lie with the magicians, who tend to punish the arrogant, the rich, the foreign, and the overbearing, and support the downtrodden and the lowly. These figures are protectors, especially with regard to the harsh authorities and the dastardly wiles of Old Nick. While the Devil is always at hand in these stories, he is also easily tricked by these figures, who at the end of their eventful lives tend to go to heaven rather than to hell, although this is sometimes a matter of dispute. Evidently most forms of magic in the Icelandic mind were protective and based on Christian knowledge rather than deemed offensive or Satanic.

Perhaps the main exception to the idea of the protective magician comes in the form of the archetypal "magician of the west fjords," about whom many people in Iceland seem to have held some degree of fear, perhaps in part because the area is still comparatively isolated. Such magicians were seen as having the power to raise people, especially children, from the dead. They would then send these figures, known as *sendingar*, walking across the country to attack others. These *sendingar*, which in some legends could be replaced by flies or animals of various kinds, are really a personification of illness or disease, a little like the children in the Icelandic stories of the Black Death (see "The Wizards of the Westmann Islands"). In the Iceland of the past, many people believed that illness was caused either by something that you accidentally saw at a dangerous time such as pregnancy, or by someone else trying to exert power over you.

Most magic in Icelandic legends, however, is first and foremost a matter of "knowledge," something echoed by one of the words for magical power: *fjölkynngi*, which literally means "many forms of knowledge." In Icelandic belief, this knowledge was essentially a knowledge of words and writing, something reflected by the stories of the Black School and the magic books possessed by people like Sæmundur and Séra (Reverend) Eiríkur of Vogsós (see the eponymous story). This feature has early roots, and is reflected in the mentions of rune magic in the sagas and Eddic poems, and in the early idea that poetry had magical power. There is also a strong possibility that people were influenced by the image of the loud-voiced, black-clad Lutheran priest who had come among them from elsewhere after having gained a knowledge of strange languages in a distant school. As he stood aloft in the pulpit, he would regularly gesture toward his big black book as he held forth fiery sermons about the Devil, a Devil that he (alone?) could witness lurking at this very moment among the timorous Icelandic congregation that stared up at him in awe. The ideas of knowledge and poetry bestowing supernatural power are well reflected in those Icelandic legends that tell of scholars or poets being the most likely people to be able to "lay" a ghost or the Devil, thereby taking the same role as that played by the blacksmith in other countries.

The Devil himself, though, is rarely a great threat in the Icelandic legends. He is more an easily outwitted comic figure, except in those cases where figures like the student Loftur attempt to go too far in their quest for knowledge (see "Loftur the Enchanter"). In general, the common view of the Devil and other Christian figures and the position of the Icelanders with regard to them is probably most fairly depicted in the tale of "The Soul of My Man Jón" in Jacqueline Simpson's *Icelandic Folktales and Legends*, where a loving Icelandic wife manages to slip the spirit of her blasphemous husband into Heaven past Peter, Paul, Mary, and Jesus.

The greatest threat to the Icelanders, however, was posed by the dead. Even today, many Icelanders believe strongly in ghosts, spirits, and the influence of the dead in their daily lives. In one sense, this is related to their deep-rooted sense of family and the whole range of family relationships. In another, it is connected to their awareness of how the dead live on among them not only in their memories and physical objects, but also in the names they bear. (Most Icelanders do not have surnames, but are simply described as being the son or daughter of their father; for example "Jónsson" or "Jónsdóttir" if their father was named Jón.) And the belief in the dead continuing to walk goes back to pre-Christian times, ghosts having a key role to play in early sagas like Eyrbyggja saga and Grettis saga.

Various types of ghosts appear in Icelandic legends. Some, especially those in experience legends, appear briefly in fact or in dream at the time of their deaths. (It might be noted that many Icelanders still have a deep belief in dreams—in their meanings, and as a means of gaining contact with the supernatural, either the dead or the *huldufólk*.) Sometimes they come to announce that they have passed on, while at other times they materialize in order to give final messages or requests. Other ghosts, like the Deacon of Myrká in the legend of the same name, are drawn back by love, money, or unfinished business. Still others walk the landscape because they have been awoken by magicians and not put back to sleep. These figures that have been summoned up frequently join forces with the spirits of those who have died of exposure after being turned away by a farm owner on a cold winter night to become so-called family *fylgjur*, or followers. Such spirits, like the famous figure of Thorgeir's Bull, tend to attach themselves to specific areas or specific people, usually the ones (or the family of those) to whom they were originally directed. Such family spirits are generally referred to as *mórar* (earth-reds) and *skottur* (tassels). The first name, used for male spirits of this kind, was a common color of clothes in earlier times, and also a color closely connected to the supernatural in Iceland. The latter name, used for female *fylgjur*, refers to a regular feature of women's caps.

As noted above, many of these Icelandic ghosts come back for retribution. This feature applies in particular to those ghosts that appear in some of the saddest Icelandic legends (also well-known elsewhere in the Scandinavian countries), namely those accounts concerning unwanted or illegitimate children who have been murdered or left out to die by their mothers and come back to haunt them and/or the areas of their deaths. These spirits are said not to be able to rest; they need either a name or some form of Christian burial to become part of the society of the dead. Legends like "Mother Mine Don't Weep, Weep" give expression to the guilt felt by the mothers, who would always have been aware where the bodies of their dead children lay buried. Equally painful is the awareness of the harsh legal system of earlier centuries that forced some women into carrying out an act of this kind to prevent themselves from being accused of adultery or incest.

One interesting feature of all of these earlier Icelandic "ghost" legends, however, is the fact the "ghosts" tend to be corporeal. In other words, they are not literally ghosts, but are the physical bodies of the dead, risen from their graves, which have come back to trouble the living, something well indicated in "The Deacon of Myrká." For this reason, we rarely find Icelandic ghosts walking through walls. Indeed, they seem to have a habit of entering into wrestling competitions with those who unwittingly encounter them. This idea of a corporeal or touchable ghost has roots in saga accounts, like those in Njáls saga and Grettis saga, telling of dead heroes heard chanting poetry in their graves or attacking grave-robbers. These ideas would have been supported by anyone who opened a Viking grave and found daily objects inside it, suggesting that the dead person had been making use of these objects.

The tales of the spirit of the *útburður*, or "borne-out child," also serve to remind us that not all Icelandic legends were meant solely to entertain or pass on facts. The evening wake or *kvöldvaka* was also in many ways a form of school for those who listened. In this sense, legends could also serve as a complement to the readings from the Bible heard alongside them. Indeed, many of them had their roots in sermons or exempla, moral tales or parables told by priests as part of their sermons. (Such deliberate religious influences are clearly seen in those relatively atypical legends that stress the pagan aspects of the *huldufólk* and portray their temptations and deceptions.) In short, many of the legends were designed to educate people about how to behave and how to avoid various dangers. They taught children to avoid lakes and pools and not stray too far from home. They also underlined the importance of helping your neighbor, the perils of laziness, the importance of showing respect to the dead and to the local priest, and the dangers of getting involved in drunken dances and having unwanted children. The legends were part textbook and part color that added depth to the living landscape around the farmhouse. They show us the struggle of the common people to understand the hardships that they were suffering, especially the ailments that struck them and their children (see the legends of changeling children, the Black Death, and the *sendingar*). They thus provide us with insight into the values and worldview of the common people of the Icelandic countryside in a time prior to the arrival of the electric light, telephones, and radio; prior to the appearance of the concrete blocks of apartment buildings; and prior to the evolution of Reykjavík into a modern 20th-century city after World War II.

The small first collection of Icelandic wondertales and legends, *Íslenzk Æfintýri* (Icelandic Fairy Tales), came out in 1852. It was the work of two men, librarian Jón Árnason (1819–1888) and former student and priest, Magnús Grímsson (1825–1860). In general terms, it can be said to be part of a wider movement that was taking place in Europe following the appearance of the Grimm brothers' collections of fairy tales and legends in 1812–1814. These works had already inspired similar collections in Denmark, Norway, and the Faroe Islands, and encouraged the English scholar George Stephens to launch an earnest appeal in print in 1845 for the Icelanders to do the same. Following their first modest offering, which came in direct answer to this call, Jón Árnason and Magnús Grímsson received encouragement to go further in their collection of material from the German scholar Konrad Maurer (1823–1902) and historian and philologist Jón Sigurðsson (1811–1879). Maurer had published his own collection of Icelandic legends, *Islandische Volkssagen* (Icelandic Folk Legends), in 1860. Jón Sigurðsson, however, had wider ambitions.

He is generally credited as being the father of Icelandic independence, something that was eventually achieved via peaceful and legal means in 1944, largely as a result of his solid groundwork in the late 19th century. As in Germany, Denmark, Norway, the Faroes, Ireland, and Scotland, the collection of folk materials, and especially folktales, had a central role in formulating a national image and identity, thereby playing a role in the nationalistic fights for independence during this period.

Unlike figures such as John Francis Campbell in Scotland, Lady Gregory in Ireland, and Asbjörnsen and Moe in Norway, Jón Árnason and Magnús Grímsson never travelled around the country collecting stories. While the latter certainly brought in a number of stories from his home county of Borgarfjörður, he died young before the overall task could be completed. Jón Árnason, who continued the project alone, was largely tied down to a job in the capital, Reykjavík. This meant he had to send out requests to clergymen and other scholars around the country, asking them to collect original material and send it in to him. This material was then edited to fit into two volumes, which were sent off to Konrad Maurer and Jón Sigurðsson in Germany and Denmark, where they received yet more editing. This overall three-step process naturally resulted in published legends (*Íslenzkar þjóðsögur og ævintýri* [Icelandic Folktales and Fairy Tales], Leipzig, 1862–1864) that were far from accurate records of the words spoken by the original storytellers. Of course, this was long before the time of tape recorders, so one can nonetheless expect there to be a more literary quality to the legends published by Jón Árnason than in those collected in later times by other Icelanders such as

Sigfús Sigfússon (*Íslenzkar þjóðsögur og sagnir* [Icelandic Folktales and Legends] I–XVI, 1922–1958; republished and updated 1984–1993), Þórbergur Þórðarson, and Sigurður Nordal (*Gráskinna hin meiri* [The Longer Grayskin], 1962), all of whom placed more emphasis on accurate transcriptions. Another important consideration is the fact that Jón Árnason tended to look for legends that he did not already have, thus lowering the number of variants he might have received. Furthermore, he, Maurer, and Jón Sigurðsson also regularly made conscious decisions about exactly which legends and fairy tales should go into the initial two-volume collection. Such decisions tended to be made on the basis of both quality and material.

None of this detracts from the importance of *Íslenzkar þjóðsögur og ævintýri*, which went on to inspire numerous other collections by men such as Ólafur Davíðsson, Jón Yorkelsson, Jónas Jónasson, Oddur Björnsson, Guðni Jónsson, Sigurður Nordal, Þórbergur Þórðarson, Þorsteinn Jónsson, Helgi Guðmundsson, Hannes Þorsteinsson, Valdimar Ásmundsson Arngrímur Fr. Bjarnason, and especially Sigfús Sigfússon, whose collecting work in the east of the country must make him the Icelandic equivalent of Evald Tang Kristensen in Denmark. Certainly, the material published by Jón Árnason is more literary, and certainly it has been chosen to underline a particular national image, with emphasis on links to the Icelandic sagas and on those forms of legend that most closely echo the legends published by the Grimms. Nonetheless, the entire collection of material collected by Jón Árnason and Magnús Grímsson has since been published in 1954–1961 in a total of six volumes, containing all the variants collected. Along with the work of Sigfús Sigfússon, this still represents one of the largest collections of Icelandic folktales in existence. It remains the best known of the collections and the model referred by all those who have followed in Jón Árnason's footsteps.

Today, work is going on at the University of Iceland to create a detailed database of all published and recorded Icelandic folk legends. By the summer of 2006, over 11,000 legends had been recorded, including many variants of common types and many tales of personal experience. To this database we are now adding information about almost as many legends that are contained in the sound archives of the Arnamagnean Institute in Iceland.

The figures given above underline the rich storehouse of legendary material that is available in Iceland. The main roadblock to international access is that most of this material is only available in Icelandic. Furthermore, what is translated into other languages tends to come from the first two volumes of Jón Árnason's collection, which, as noted above, does not really give a fair impression of the whole collection. It is hoped that in the future funds will be found to pay for the legend summaries contained in the database to be translated into English. Until then, readers will have to be content with collections like this one, which try to give at least a representative taste of the whole and the environment in which these legends were told.

ONE

Hidden People

The Origin of the Hidden People

At the beginning of time, God paid a visit to the first of his creations, Adam and Eve. They received him with great joy and showed him all of their possessions, including their beautiful children. God saw that their children were lovely and full of promise.

"Are there other children I have yet to meet?" God asked Eve.

"No," Eve replied.

Eve lied to God because she had not finished bathing her other children and she was ashamed to have the Almighty see them, so she hid them.

Of course, God knew she was hiding the children and rebuked her. "What you hide from my sight, I will hide from yours," he said.

The unwashed children of Adam and Eve became invisible and lived among the hills, moors, and woods. They became known as elves. Humans are the descendants of the children Eve proudly showed to God. Only when an elf desires to be seen can a person see him. Thus they are called the *huldufólk*, or "Hidden People."

Another story tells of a traveller who lost his way. He wandered for some time until he came to a hut in the woods. He knocked on the door and an old woman opened it. She invited him in and he gladly accepted.

Once inside, the traveller noticed that the house was very clean and tidy. The old woman led him to the warmest room and introduced him to her two young and beautiful daughters. The girls received the traveller with kindness, served him a good supper, and offered him a soft bed.

Later that evening, the traveller requested that one of the girls lie with him and keep him company throughout the night. His request was granted, but when he tried to kiss the girl, the hand he placed on her sank through as if she were made from mist. The man was surprised that he could see her lying beside him, but he could not touch her. "What does this mean?" he asked.

"I am a spirit," the girl replied. "When the devil made war in the heavens, he, along with his army was cast out into darkness. Those who turned their eyes to watch his fall were likewise driven out of heaven. But those who were neither for nor against him were sent to earth and commanded to live in the rocks and mountains. We are called the Hidden People or elves.

Elves can live in the company of none but their own. We do either good or evil—and whichever one we choose, we do it well. Elves have no mortal bodies, but can take on human form whenever we wish men to see us. I am one of these spirits, so there is no hope of you ever embracing me."

The traveller accepted his fate and lived to tell the rest of us his story.

Based on Jón Árnason I, 7

The Elf-woman in Childbirth

One evening, in the southeast at Oddi, a young servant girl stepped outside to collect her freshly washed laundry. It was quiet in the churchyard as she busily plucked up the clothing, folded it, and placed it in her basket.

Suddenly, a strange man appeared beside her. He told her not to be afraid and said he meant her no harm. Then he grabbed her hand and ordered her to come with him. When she resisted, he said, "If you do not come, your good luck will change to bad."

Frightened, the girl obeyed and followed him out of the churchyard. After they walked briskly for some time, a farmhouse appeared in the distance. What the girl didn't know was that the farmhouse was an illusion and she was actually approaching a small grassy knoll.

The man led her to the farmhouse door, opened it, and beckoned her to follow him down a long, dark passageway. As they walked, a cry of agony drifted down the hallway, increasing in volume as they approached the main room of the house. By the dim light of a lantern, the girl saw a woman lying on the floor, suffering and unable to give birth to her child. A very distressed old woman sat by her side.

"Go to my wife," the man said. "Help her give birth to the child."

As the girl approached, the old woman moved away. Kneeling beside the distraught mother, the girl gently ran her hands up and down her belly, seeking out the form of the baby. She quickly figured out the problem and helped the woman deliver her child.

Moments after his child was born, the man came back into the room and handed the girl a glass bottle. He asked her to put some of the contents into the child's eyes, but warned her not to get any in her own. The girl obeyed, but once she was finished with the child, she couldn't resist putting a drop on her finger and gently touching one of her eyes. Immediately, she saw a small crowd of people watching her from the far end of the room.

Not noticing what she had done, the man took the bottle, thanked the girl for her help, and promised that she would live a very lucky life. Then he placed a bolt of beautiful cloth in her apron and led her back to the churchyard. After bidding her a fond farewell, the man left. The girl collected her laundry and returned home.

The girl often bragged that she could see the Hidden People. No one believed her, but neither could they deny that her luck had greatly improved. For example, whenever she saw the Hidden People piling their hay into mounds, she ordered her hay mounded too. And sure enough, even though the skies had been clear for days, it would begin to rain. While the others scrambled to protect their hay, hers was safe and dry.

The following winter, the priest's wife died and he chose the servant girl as his new wife. One day while at the market with her husband, she saw the elf-man, whose wife she had helped, buying goods from a Hidden People's merchant. She happily walked over and greeted him saying, "Good luck go with you, friend! I thank you for your kindness last time we met."

Before the girl realized her mistake, the man walked over to her, licked his finger, and swiped it across her eyes. At once, her ability to see the Hidden People or anything that they were doing was gone.

Based on Jón Árnason I, 16–17

The Grateful Elf-woman

One day the kind wife of a peasant man had a dream. She dreamed that a *huldukona*, or elf-woman, was standing by her bedside. The woman desperately needed to feed her child and begged for two quarts of milk a day for a month. The elf-woman asked her to place the bowl in a specific spot in the house. The peasant woman's heart was stirred by the plea and she promised to supply the milk.

When the good woman woke, she remembered her dream. She quickly placed a bowl of milk in the elf-woman's chosen spot and left it there. When she returned later in the day, the bowl was empty. Every day she faithfully filled the bowl and every day she was pleased to find that the milk was gone.

A month later, the peasant woman had another dream. The elf-woman again appeared at her bedside, offering thanks for her kindness and begging her to accept a gift that she would find in her bed the following morning. Then, as suddenly as she appeared, the woman vanished.

In the morning, the peasant woman reached beneath her pillow and pulled out a beautiful silver belt, with intricately detailed designs carved into it. The promised gift from a grateful elf-woman.

Based on Jón Árnason I, 10–11

The Magic Scythe

It happened one day that a hard-working man left his home in the south to journey across a mountain to the north of the country. It was the hay-cutting season and he went in search of work. After packing his horses and saddling his mount, he began the long journey. For many hours he followed a path, snaking its way higher and higher into the mountain.

Suddenly, a thick mist surrounded him. He lost sight of the path and in confusion lost his way. A freezing rain began to fall, and fearing to go any further, he decided to set up camp. After securing the horses, he crawled into his tent, opened his pack, and prepared an evening meal.

He was happily eating his supper when all of a sudden the tent flaps opened and a fierce, brown dog slipped inside. The mangy, wet, and dirty animal frightened the man. He quickly shoved food toward the dog, hoping it would devour the bread and meat instead of him. The dog snatched the food, eating everything the man offered. When the dog was finished, it left the tent and ran off into the mist.

The man contemplated the sudden arrival of a dog so high in the mountains. Why was it there, in such a wild and barren place? Finding no reasonable answer, he forgot about the dog, finished his meal and settled in for the night. Using his saddle as a pillow, he quickly fell into a deep sleep.

At midnight, the man had a dream. An old woman entered his tent, stood by his side, and said, "Thank you, my good man, for showing kindness to my daughter. No reward would be payment enough for your compassion. I am placing a scythe under your pillow. It is all I have to offer. Do not look upon it with scorn for it will prove useful to you. It can cut down anything you set before it. But I must warn you. Never put it into the fire to temper it. Sharpen it as you see fit, but never by fire." And she vanished from sight.

The man awoke refreshed and ready to face a new day. He emerged from the tent, happy to see the mist gone and the sun shining warm and bright. After gathering his supplies, he struck the tent and loaded the packhorses. When he was finished, he turned to saddle his riding horse. He lifted the saddle from the ground, and discovered a small scythe blade lying beneath it. The blade was worn and rusty, but at the sight of it, the man remembered his dream. Picking it up, he placed it in his pack and began his journey. He quickly found the pathway across the mountain and hastily made his way to the populated areas of the north.

When he finally arrived in the north, one week of harvest had passed. He journeyed from house to house, searching for a job, but every farmer had enough workers in their employ. Along the way, he learned of an old woman in the district who always started her harvest a week later than everyone else did. She seldom employed workers, but always managed to finish the harvest by the end of the season. Her neighbors thought that she was very rich and a witch, skilled in the art of magic.

The other laborers suggested that the man approach the old woman and ask for work. They warned him of her strange habits and said that on rare occasions, she would employ a worker. But they cautioned that somehow, she managed never to pay for the labor. With their warnings ringing in his ears, and no other jobs available, the man decided to take a chance. He approached the old woman's house and offered his services for the harvest. She accepted his offer, saying he could work for one week but should expect no wages. "Unless," she said, "you cut down more grass in the whole week than I can rake on the last day. If you succeed, I will pay your wages."

After agreeing to the woman's terms, the man began to mow her fields using the scythe that the elf-woman from his dream had given him. All day long he cut the grass, and to his amazement, the scythe stayed sharp. The man worked hard and had no complaints, for the old woman was kind to him.

On Friday, the fifth day, the man entered the forge near the old woman's house. Once inside, he noticed a large number of rakes, many scythe handles, and a pile of blades. He was very curious about why the old woman had collected so many of these things.

That night while he slept the elf-woman again appeared to him in a dream. She said, "Although you have mowed many fields, the old woman will easily rake it all in one day. And if she does, she will drive you away without paying your wages. When you see that she is beating you, go to the forge and gather as many scythe handles as you can carry. Fix blades to each handle and take them to an uncut field. Lay them on the ground and watch what happens." After she spoke, she disappeared.

In the morning, the man got up and set to work mowing another field. At six o'clock, the old witch arrived, carrying five rakes. She said, "Indeed, you have mowed a large amount of hay!" She laid her rakes along the edge of the hayfield, keeping one in her hands. She started raking and to the man's amazement, gathered huge amounts of hay. Then he noticed the other rakes. Of their own accord, with no hand to guide them, they raked in as much hay as the old woman did.

The man continued to mow as fast as he could, but by noon, he realized that the old witch was quickly raking all the hay that he had cut down. Realizing that he could lose all his wages, the man ran to the forge. He gathered several scythe handles and quickly fixed a blade to each one. He carried them to an uncut field and laid them on the ground. To his delight, the scythes set to work. Without a hand upon them, they cut grass so quickly that the rakes could not keep up.

And so it went. All day long, the scythes cut hay, staying well ahead of the old witch and her rakes. As night fell, the old witch told the man to gather up his scythes while she collected the rakes. She said to him, "You are smarter than I thought you were. You know more than I do. That is good—and you may stay with me for as long as you wish."

The man spent the summer working for the old witch. They got along and together mowed and raked vast amounts of hay. When autumn came, she sent him home with a large amount of money in his pockets.

He returned to the witch's farm the next summer and the summer after that. Each year, he returned home at the end of the season with a great deal of money.

After several years, the man bought his own farm and stayed in the south of Iceland. His neighbors thought he was an honest man, a good fisherman and a talented worker, who excelled in whatever he did. Each year at harvest time, the man always cut his own hay. He never used any scythe but the one the elf-woman gave him on the mountain. And each year, he finished his work well before his neighbors.

One summer, while the man was out fishing, a neighbor arrived at his house. He asked the farmer's wife if he could use the farmer's scythe. He had lost his own and wished to finish harvesting his crop. The wife searched for a scythe, but could only find the one her husband favored above all others. With great reluctance, she handed him the scythe and begged him not to temper it with fire, for she knew that her husband never did. The man promised and went on his way.

The neighbor bound a handle to the scythe and went out to his hayfield. He swiped at the grass, swinging back and forth until sweat poured down his face. No matter how hard he tried, not a single blade of grass fell to the ground. Angry, the man tried to sharpen the scythe but that didn't help. It wouldn't cut the grass. Finally, ignoring his neighbor's plea, he took the scythe into his forge to temper it.

But as soon as the flames touched the blade, the steel melted like wax, leaving behind nothing but a small pile of ashes.

Dismayed, the neighbor raced back to the farmer's house and told the wife what had happened. Frightened and ashamed, the wife realized her mistake. She should never have loaned the scythe to anyone. Her husband was very fond of it and he would surely be angry when he found out what she had done.

And angry he was! When he returned home and heard what had happened to his scythe, angry words poured out of his mouth, condemning his wife for loaning out something that was not hers. Luckily for them both, his anger soon ended and he adjusted to life without his magic scythe.

Based on Jón Árnason I, 12–14

The Elf-steeple

Hundreds of years ago, a rich farmer lived in Sælingsdalstunga. He had several children but it is his two sons, Arnór and Sveinn, who are important to this story. Both boys were full of promise, though completely different in personality. Arnór was strong and brave, an active joyful youth. Popular among the young men of the valley, he loved rowdy outdoor sports and wild unruly games. Sveinn was gentle and timid, a quiet pensive young man.

Near the river stood a rocky hill whose majestic pinnacle earned it the name Stapi, or steeple. Arnór and the other young men often gathered to play at the foot of this hill, near the Tunga farm. In the winter, they enjoyed climbing to the pinnacle of Stapi and sliding down on the hard packed snow. With Arnór in the lead, they hauled their sleighs to the top and, with shouts of merriment and screams of fear, raced to the bottom and out onto the river flats. Night after night, as twilight enveloped Stapi, their joyful voices echoed across the valley.

Sveinn spent most of his time in church. He seldom joined the young men at play, but loved to wander near the foot of the hill where it was quiet and peaceful. These quiet wanderings soon led to rumors among the people in the valley. Rumors flared each New Year's Eve when Sveinn disappeared and no one could find him. Everyone said that he spent the night in the company of the elf-folk who lived inside the mountain.

Whenever Arnór returned from an evening of raucous play, Sveinn begged him to be quieter when playing games on the hillside. "If you didn't quiet down, Arnór," he said, "you will be responsible for whatever happens."

But Arnór refused to listen, ignoring his brother's warnings. "I don't care if the elves are bothered by our noise," he said. "We are having fun on that hill and don't intend to stop."

One New Year's Eve, Sveinn disappeared as usual. But this time, he stayed away for longer than ever before. Worried, Arnór decided to search for him. He jokingly said, "He must be enjoying the company of his friends, the elves. I'll go to Stapi and find him."

Arnór set off on foot in search of his brother. An overcast sky blocked out the moon and stars, forcing him to walk in darkness. When Arnór reached the side of the hill facing the Tunga farm, the rocks opened up to reveal rows and rows of brightly lit lamps. From inside, he heard beautiful music and exquisite voices raised in song. The elves were holding their midnight Mass.

Walking between the rows of lights, Arnór approached the doors of a church. They were open wide, revealing a vast crowd of worshipers gathered around a priest. The priest was dressed in splendid robes and stood near an altar, surrounded by hundreds of burning candles.

As Arnór moved closer, he spotted his brother kneeling at the altar. The priest stood over Sveinn, resting his hands on his head and murmuring strange words. Others dressed in similar sacred robes stood nearby. In amazement, Arnór realized that his brother was being initiated into the elven priesthood.

In fear Arnór cried out, "Sveinn, come with me. Your life is in danger!"

His cry startled Sveinn. He jumped up and turned toward his brother's voice. At that moment, when Sveinn was about to run, the priest cried out, "Shut the church doors! We must punish the man who entered this holy place and disturbed our sacred ceremony."

The priest then turned to Sveinn and said, "Although it is your brother's fault, you must leave this place. Your response to a brother's cry proves that you love him more than our sacred ceremony. When your eyes next observe me standing in my robes at this altar, you will die."

A frightened Arnór watched as several in the crowd lifted his brother high in the air, moved toward the church vault and disappeared from sight. At the exact moment Sveinn disappeared, the peal of church bells vibrated through the room. The crowd surged toward the still opened doorway, shoving and pushing to get out.

Arnór raced ahead of the crowd, out of the church and into the night. As fast as he could, he ran toward home. Then suddenly he heard the clamor of elven feet and the thunder of elven horses. Above the noise, he heard a voice cry out:

Ride! Ride! Ride on!
The slopes are dark, the path is dim;
He flees away, chase after him.
Let us, with our enchantment spread
Confusion o'er his feet and head.
To ensure that he never may
See the dawn of another day.
Ride! Ride! Ride on!

The elves positioned themselves between Arnór and the farm, forcing him to turn around and run in the opposite direction. Blindly he ran, scaling hills, climbing rocks, and struggling through twisted and tangled plants. When he reached a slope east of the farm, his strength failed. He fell to the ground, and the elves rode over him. The hooves of their horses bruised and battered Arnor's body, leaving him at the brink of death.

While Arnór fought for his life, Sveinn returned to the farmhouse. The rest of the family was preparing for bed when he arrived. They asked where he had been, but Sveinn refused to answer. Instead, he roused the servants and begged them to organize a search for his brother.

All through the night, they searched, but no one could find Arnór.

In the early hours of the morning, a farmer from Laugar was travelling eastward on his way to Tunga for a morning worship service. He found Arnór lying on the side of the hill where the elves had left him. The farmer knelt beside the dying man. He listened intently as, with the last of his strength, Arnór whispered his story. When the farmer bent to lift him up, Arnór begged to be left alone. Since there was no chance of recovery, he wanted to die where he lay. To this day, that hill is called Banabrekkur, the slopes of death.

Following Arnor's death, Sveinn became sullen, silent, and even stranger than before. He never ventured near Stapi nor looked in its direction. He turned away from worldly things and began to focus on becoming a monk. He shut himself away in the monastery at Helgafell, studied hard, and became the most learned in the brotherhood.

Sveinn also had a beautiful voice. It was said that when he sang the Mass, even the angels listened. No one was his equal, and everyone who knew him felt he was not of this world.

In the years that followed, Sveinn's father continued to live at Tunga farm. When he was well into old age, he fell sick. Knowing that his final days were near, he yearned to see his son. He sent word to the monastery, begging Sveinn to return home.

Although it was Holy Week, Sveinn immediately prepared to go to his father's bedside. When he was ready to depart, the other monks gathered to bid him safe journey. To each of them Sveinn sadly said, "May all be well with you forever. For there is a chance I will not return to you alive."

Sveinn arrived at Tunga farm on the Saturday before Easter. When he reached his father's bedside, he found him weak and barely able to speak. The old man begged his son to carry out his dying wish—to hear him sing the Mass on Easter Sunday. Sveinn was reluctant to grant the wish, but finally agreed on one condition. The church doors must remain firmly closed throughout the entire service. Sveinn's life would depend on it.

On Easter morning, the dying old man's servants carried him into the church and firmly closed the doors. Many of the worshipers thought this strange, but figured it was because Sveinn did not want to look out toward Stapi and remember his brother's death.

Sveinn took his place on the steps of the altar. Dressed in priestly robes, he sweetly sang the Mass. His beautiful voice filled the church, leaving the congregation speechless. In awe, the people sank to their knees in worship, barely able to breathe because of the wondrous sound. At the close of the service, Sveinn turned to the people and with outstretched arms proclaimed his blessing upon them. Suddenly, a gust of wind raced in from the west and struck the church. The doors burst open, ripping themselves from their hinges, and falling heavily to the ground.

Startled, the people turned to see what had happened. Framed by the doorway, they watched as the hillside of Stapi opened up to reveal rows and rows of burning lamps. They turned back toward the altar only to find Sveinn dead on the floor, and his father's body nearby.

The farmer, who found Arnór's body on the hillside years earlier, happened to attend that mass. He told the people Arnór's story. And when he was finished, everyone understood that the elven priest's prediction had come true. As Sveinn had stood at the altar and the doors had come crashing down, his eyes had looked straight into the eyes of the elven priest. They both had recited the benediction and then Sveinn had died.

Father and son were buried on the same day.

Later, the people of the parish met to discuss what happened that day. They decided to move their church from where it stood on the hilltop near the Tunga farm to a hollow beside the stream. This position put the farm between the church and Stapi. Never again could a priest stand at the altar and look west toward the Elf-steeple.

Based on Jón Árnason I, 32–35

The Father of Eighteen Elves

It was a warm autumn day during harvest season when a strange thing happened. A farmer took his entire household out to the fields to gather hay. Only his wife, the mistress of the house, stayed behind to finish her chores and watch over their young son. The child was three years old, a strong and healthy lad. An only child, he spoke well for his age and everyone felt he was destined for a promising future. And, of course, he was his parents' pride and joy.

The mistress of the house was a busy woman. While she worked, her young son was always by her side. But that day, when it came time for her to wash the milk buckets, she left the lad in the doorway of the farmhouse to play. She left him alone only long enough to wash the buckets in the stream and set them out to dry.

When she returned a short time later, she spoke to the child and a bewildering thing happened. The boy shrieked and howled, making vicious and ugly sounds, quite unlike his usual kind and sweet-tempered self. The mother tried to reason with him, but he remained willful and moody.

The outbursts continued for quite some time. The lad stopped growing and he started acting like a complete imbecile. Everyone feared he had lost his senses.

In desperation, the mother sought guidance from a neighbor woman who was thought to be very wise and skilled in the ways of the world. The woman asked her several questions. When did the change in the child occur? What did the mother think might have caused the change? The grieving mother told her everything that happened, answering each question as best she could.

The wise woman listened intently, considering every aspect of the story. Finally, she said, "Have you considered that the child who now lives in your home is a changeling? I have no doubt that he was changed during the moments you left him alone at the cottage door."

"I don't know," the mother replied. "Is there some way I can find out for sure? I must know the truth."

"I can help you," the wise woman said. "Here's what I want you to do. Place the child in front of something strange—something he has never seen before. Then leave him alone, but stay close by so you can hear what he says and see what he does. If he thinks he is alone, he will speak. Listen carefully. If he says anything strange or suspicious you will know that he is a changeling. Once you know for sure, beat him without mercy and see what happens next."

With hope in her heart, the mother thanked the wise woman for her advice and returned home. As soon as she arrived at the cottage, she set a plan in motion. First she took a small cooking pot and placed it in the middle of the kitchen floor. Then she gathered several broom sticks and tied them together, end to end. At one end, she tied a porridge spoon and placed it in the pot. The other end, she shoved up the chimney.

When she was finished with her strange device, she brought the child into the kitchen and placed him on the floor. She left the room, but stayed close by, peeking through a crack in the cottage door. From her hiding spot, she could see and hear everything that happened in the kitchen.

The boy stared at the contraption for several minutes. Then he stood up and toddled around and around the pot, examining it from every angle. "By the white of my whiskers!" he said. "I am an old man, and the father of eighteen elves, but never have I seen such a long spoon in such a tiny pot."

At the moment he said those words, the mother rushed into the room. With a birch switch, she began beating the changeling. She whipped him until he kicked and screamed and hollered. Remembering the wise woman's advice, the mother continued to whip the changeling. Suddenly, in the midst of all the hollering, a strange woman entered the kitchen. In her arms she was cuddling a sweet and charming boy.

"See how differently we act?" she said. "I love and care for your son while you beat and abuse my husband!" And with those words, she passed the child to his mother, reached for the changeling's hand and disappeared.

Despite this traumatic incident, the lad grew into manhood and fulfilled all the promises of his youth.

Based on Jón Árnason I, 43–44

The Girl at the Shieling

A long time ago, a priest from the north of the country owned several summer pastures high in the hills. Each summer his cattle and sheep were herded to these pastures to graze. And each summer the priest sent along a housekeeper to tend the house and cook meals for the herdsmen.

Years passed and eventually the priest's only child, an adopted daughter, became housekeeper at the shieling. A girl of great beauty and skill, she was considered the best match in all of the north. Many wealthy men asked for her hand in marriage, but she refused them all.

One day, the priest decided to have a serious talk with his daughter about marriage. He reminded her that he was an old man and the day would eventually come when he could no longer care for her. He pleaded with her to consider at least one of her many marriage proposals.

Greatly distressed by his words, the girl told her father that she had no interest in marrying anyone. She begged him to be content with the way things were. And furthermore, she said, marriage was always filled with bad luck.

Saddened by her response, the priest gave up trying to convince his daughter to marry.

The winter passed, and soon the villagers began to notice that the girl was putting on weight. By spring, she was quite heavy and appeared to be pregnant. Her father urged her to confide in him. He felt that she should not go to the shieling that summer, for it was no place to give birth to a child.

The girl vehemently denied being pregnant. She said that there was nothing wrong with her and she would see to her housekeeping the same as she had all the summers before.

Frustrated by her deceit, the priest went to his herdsmen and ordered them to watch over his daughter and never let the girl out of their sight. As long as she was at the shieling, someone must be with her.

The day finally came for the move to the shieling, and the girl seemed unusually happy.

Spring passed into summer and the men faithfully kept watch, never leaving the girl alone, not for a single moment.

One evening in late summer, one of the shepherds discovered that all the sheep and cows were gone! Everyone hurried into the hills in search of the missing animals except the housekeeper—she stayed behind, alone. The herdsmen searched all night, and near dawn they finally found the animals.

When they returned to the shieling, the girl was busy with her work, but brisker in her movements and lighter on her feet. As the weeks passed, they noticed that she lost her plumpness. Since there was no baby, the men figured that she must have suffered from some kind of swelling and not a pregnancy.

In the autumn, the girl returned to her father's house. When the priest saw that his daughter was much slimmer than when she left, he called in the herdsmen and asked if they had disobeyed him and left the girl alone. They told him the truth. Only once was she left alone. The night when all the herds went missing and every man was needed to find them. The priest was angry at them and wished bad luck on all of them for disobeying his orders.

The following winter, a farmer from the area asked for the girl's hand in marriage. The girl was very unhappy about the proposal but her father insisted that she marry him. The farmer had inherited his father's farm that spring and his mother ran the house for him. He was a fine man and everyone thought well of him.

Although the girl objected, the marriage was arranged and the ceremony set for later in the spring. On her wedding day, before she put on her bridal dress, the girl went to her betrothed and said, "I do not wish to marry you. But since I must, I demand that you agree to one condition. You must promise to never allow strangers to lodge with us during the winter without first telling me. If you don't tell me, things will go bad for you."

The farmer gave her his promise and they were married.

The wedding feast went as planned and the girl returned home with her new husband. She took over the running of their home, but her heart was not in it. Her husband pampered her and would not allow her to work very hard. But no matter how hard he tried, the girl remained sullen and unhappy.

In the summer, the farmer's wife remained at home while the rest of the household worked in the hayfields. Her mother-in-law stayed behind to keep her company and help with the housework. During quiet times of the day, the two women sat spinning wool and knitting garments. The old woman tried to entertain her daughter-in-law with amusing stories.

One day, when the old woman ended her story, she asked her daughter-in-law to tell one of her own. The daughter-in-law replied that she didn't know any. But the old woman insisted, until finally she agreed to tell her the only story she knew. Here is the tale she told:

"Once there was a farm girl who worked as a housekeeper at the shieling. Near the house were rocky cliffs where she loved to go for quiet walks. A man, a member of the Hidden Folk, lived inside the cliffs. He and the girl became acquainted and soon fell deeply in love. He was a good and kind man who granted the girl her every wish.

"Eventually, the girl discovered that she was going to have a child. When the master of the household accused her of being pregnant, she denied it.

"When she returned to the shieling the following spring, the girl realized that the master had ordered his herdsmen never to leave her alone. They obeyed his orders except for one night, when all their animals went missing and every person was needed for the search.

"While everyone was gone, the girl went into labor. The elf-man appeared at her side and helped her through the ordeal. After the baby was born, he cut the cord, washed the child, and wrapped it in a warm blanket. Then, just before he left with the child, he offered the girl a drink from his flask. It was the sweetest drink I ever—" And at that moment, the girl dropped her ball of wool. She bent down to retrieve it, and continued her story.

"—that she had ever tasted, is what I meant to say. After drinking the liquid, the girl suffered no pain from the child's birth. The man disappeared with the child and the girl never saw him again. The girl was eventually forced to marry another man. To this day she pines bitterly for her lost lover and child. And from that time on, she has never had a happy day. And so ends my story."

The mother-in-law thanked her daughter-in-law for the story and took great care to remember it. Time passed and the farmer's wife continued to be sad but treated her husband with kindness.

One summer, when the mowing was almost done, two men walked up to the farmer in his field. One of the men was tall and the other short. Both wore broad-brimmed hats that covered their faces. The taller one asked if the farmer would allow them to work and live with him for the winter. The farmer said that he must first ask his wife. He never promised lodging to anyone without consulting her.

The tall man said that he thought that was ridiculous. How was it that such a fine and masterful man could be so henpecked? Could he not make up his own mind on such a little matter? Two men requesting work in exchange for room and board for one winter—such a simple request!

The farmer's pride made him give in and promise them winter lodging.

Later that evening, the strangers arrived at the farmer's house. He assigned them a room in a building on the outskirts of the farm and told them to stay there. Then he went to his wife and told her about the two men. She was very unhappy and accused him of not fulfilling the first and only promise she had ever asked of him. Since he had decided on his own to allow the men to lodge with them, he would be responsible for their care for the entire winter.

The summer passed and later in the autumn, the farmer and his wife decided to go to Holy Communion.

It was a custom in those days, and a long-standing custom in Iceland, that anyone who planned to go to Communion would first go to every person in their household, kiss them and beg their forgiveness for any offense. Until this time, the farmer's wife had avoided the two lodgers, never even letting them see her face. And likewise, on this occasion, she did not go and greet them.

So the farmer and his wife set out for the church. As soon as they were beyond the fence, he asked her, "You did greet our lodgers, didn't you?"

"No," she said, resolutely.

"But how could you commit such a great sin?" the farmer asked in astonishment.

"You have shown in many ways that you do not care for me," she said. "First you take in these men without consulting me and now you force me to kiss them. Fine—I will obey you. You will regret forcing this issue for my very life is threatened. And yours as well."

The farmer's wife turned away from her husband and walked back to the farm. She was gone a very long time and finally the worried farmer decided to search for her. He went to where he thought she would be— at the lodger's room. When he arrived at the room, he found his wife and the tall lodger dead on the floor. They were wrapped in each other's arms—dead from grief. The shorter man was standing over them, weeping. When the farmer entered the room, the short man disappeared and no one ever saw him again.

The farmer's mother retold her daughter-in-law's story. The people in the region felt that the tall stranger was surely the elf-lover from the shieling and the short one was their son.

Based on Jón Árnason I, 63–66

Katla's Dream

A very long time ago in the land west of Reykhólar, a powerful chieftain named Már was married to a kind and noble woman named Katla. Katla loved her husband and happily spent her days tending to his every need.

One day, Már decided to go to a meeting of the Althingi (parliament). Since he would be away for several days, Katla stayed behind to tend to their household. On one of the mornings, Katla rose early to attend to her daily chores. But, instead of feeling energetic and ready to face a new day, she felt strangely exhausted and drowsy. She returned to her bed and immediately fell into a deep sleep.

At noon, Katla's attendants called for her. When they received no reply, the women tried to wake her. Katla did not respond. Frightened and fearing that she was dead, the attendants raced to the rooms of Katla's foster-father and begged him to come and help. The old man tried in vain to rouse Katla, but she remained in a deep sleep.

Discouraged, the old man sat next to Katla's couch. "She is not dead," he said to the attendants. "The flame of life is still flickering in her chest. But like you, I can not wake her."

For the next four days and nights, Katla's father remained at her side, keeping careful watch. On the fifth day, Katla woke. She returned to her daily activities, but appeared to be extremely sad and depressed. Fearing they might distress her further, everyone in the household left her alone and did not ask any questions.

A few days later, Már returned from the Althingi to find a wife very different from the one he left behind. Katla refused to greet him. She did not offer her usual love and affection nor show any joy at his safe return.

Sad and confused, Már tried to figure out what had happened during his absence. He spoke to each of Katla's attendants, but none of the women could answer his questions. They each repeated the story about how she had slept for four days and four nights. Everyone agreed that following her long sleep she became sad and withdrawn.

After speaking to all the attendants and finding no logical answers, Már approached Katla. He sat down with her and begged her to tell him what had happened during that long sleep. After reassuring her that he wanted to share her burden, he convinced her that she would feel better if she told him what was making her so sad.

Katla told him her story:

"As you already know," Katla said. "One morning while you were away, I fell into a deep sleep. A woman appeared at my bedside. She was beautiful and richly dressed. She spoke sweetly to me and said that she lived nearby on the Thverá farm. She asked if I would walk part of the way back to the farm with her and I agreed.

"I rose from my bed, and in the exact spot where I had been lying, she placed her gloves. 'These will take your place while you are away,' she said.

"We walked for some time until we came to the shore of a large lake. Its surface was clear and smooth as glass. A gaily painted boat was moored nearby. After the woman thanked me for walking with her, I wished her a fond farewell.

"Then suddenly she stretched out her hand and pleaded, 'Will you not say goodbye to Alvör?'

"As I reached toward her, she grasped my hand and leaped into the boat, dragging me along with her. Before I realized what was happening, Alvör (for that was the woman's name) was swiftly rowing the boat toward a small island in the middle of the lake.

"I realized that she had some kind of power over me. I was terrified and helpless to defy her. She said that Fate was compelling her to treat me in this way. She tried to calm my fears by reassuring me that eventually I would return safely home.

"As we approached the island, a castle loomed before us. It was the most beautiful castle in the world. More beautiful than anything I had ever seen.

"Alvör said, 'This castle is mine.'

"The boat reached shore and we disembarked. Alvör grasped my hand and led me into the castle. She immediately took me to her chambers where her ladies-in-waiting sat around a bath filled with sweet water. After I had bathed, Alvör led me to a down-filled bed surrounded by richly colored curtains. One of the ladies handed me a glass of wine that tasted rare and wonderful. I was exhausted, and with the help of the wine and the soft bed, I soon fell fast asleep.

"I woke some time later and was amazed to discover a cloak, embroidered in pure gold, lying next to me. One of the ladies brought me other garments, including a dress with the same gold designs. After I was dressed, Alvör placed her own fur-lined velvet cloak, daintily stitched in gold, over my shoulders.

"Besides these beautiful garments, Alvör gave me five rings of red gold, a golden band for my hair, and a very expensive belt. As I stood before her, attired in this finery, she begged me to accept all the treasures as a gift from her.

"Alvör then requested that six of her ladies accompany us to the dining hall. We entered a magnificently decorated room. Each wall was covered with cloth of finely spun gold. On each table sat silver vessels overflowing with food, silver flagons filled with ale, and gold inlaid chalices brimming with mulled wine. Sitting around every table were splendidly dressed ladies and handsome men.

"At the head of the room stood a throne, and on a couch beside it lay a man dressed in the finest silk. Alvör approached the sleeping man and shook him awake.

"He opened his eyes, sat up and said, 'Why have you awakened me? Do you bring good news? Is Katla here?'

"He searched the crowd and spotted me. Immediately, he rose from his couch and strode across the room. Gently taking my hand, he led me to the throne. After bidding me be seated, he sat down beside me.

"Alvör pointed to us and cried out, 'Behold! The bride and bridegroom!' At her words, everyone in the room shouted for joy. A celebration began and continued until nightfall.

"Later that evening, Alvör told me that I must spend the night with Kári. I was filled with anger and replied, 'Never! I will not do this. I love my husband Már too much to ever share a bed with another man.'

"She replied, 'If you refuse, great evil will cling to you for the rest of your life. Make a wise choice and consent.'

"I was frightened and alone. No one in the castle

would come to my rescue. I was a sheep amid a pack of wolves.

"The ladies led me back to Alvör's chamber, to the bed I had slept in earlier that day. Kári soon arrived and offered me all his riches, gold, and jewels, if I would choose to love him. I told him that his love was hopeless, but he would not listen to me. Then he brought a chalice of wine and after first tasting it himself, ordered me to drink it.

"As I drank the wine, he said, 'I would rather die than see you unhappy. Be comforted. You will soon return to your home.' With those reassuring words, he lay down beside me.

"I do not know if it was his constant pleas, his beautiful person, or the effects of the wine, but I soon accepted his love. Although my heart was breaking, we stayed together two days and two nights.

"At the end of the two days, Kári said, 'You will soon give birth to a son. Please name him after me and give him this belt and knife as a gift from a father he will never know.

"He showed me a golden belt and a knife with a finely crafted handle. He placed the gifts, along with my clothes and jewels into a bag and begged me to take them home with me.

"'Although it will be hard,' he said. 'It is your duty to share what happened here with your husband. Ask him to build you a new home at Thverá, between the two small hills where the birds gather. Those hills hide great stores of money. A gift from me to you. Together, you and Már will raise a large and prosperous family.'

"He rose from my side and sadly said, 'My life is at an end. You will never set eyes on me again.'

"Taking me by the hand, Alvör led me from the room. As I walked down the hallway, a loud cracking sound echoed through the building. I turned and saw Kári dead, on the floor. The sound had been his heart breaking with love for me and sorrow at losing me.

"Alvör rowed the boat back across the lake and accompanied me into the house. She removed the gloves from my bed. 'I wish you well,' she said. 'Although I will forever grieve the loss of my son, I hope you will enjoy your treasures and build a happy life.' And with those words, she disappeared."

Katla begged Már to forgive her and reassured him that her love remained true and strong. Már asked to see the gifts and Katla showed him all the treasures she had brought from Alvör's castle.

Late the following winter, Katla gave birth to a beautiful son. Már named the boy Kári, as his elf father had wished. Although Katla could not love the boy with a true mother's love, Már doted on him as any true father would.

Már found the mounds of money hidden where Kári had promised and built a new farm at Thverá. A year later, Katla gave birth to another son. She named him Ari.

The years passed. Már and Katla loved each other dearly and happily lived out their lives together. Their son Ari eventually became a great chieftain and fathered a long line of descendants.

Kári settled in Rennudalur, married, and became a wealthy man. He studied the tides and the stars and became known throughout the county for his vast knowledge of the Hidden People.

Based on Jón Árnason I, 59–63

The Church Builder of Reynir

A long time ago in the community of Reynir, there lived a farmer who was ordered by the bishop to build a church. He chose a spot near his farmhouse and arranged for the lumber to be delivered. To the farmer's dismay, it took a long time for the wood to arrive. When it finally came, all the carpenters in the village were busy harvesting their winter hay. Sadly, the farmer feared that the new church would not be completed before winter set in.

One day, as the farmer strolled through his field, a strange man approached him and offered a casual greeting. The farmer returned the greeting, and went on worrying about how to tell the bishop that the church would not be finished on time. To the farmer's surprise, the stranger spoke up and offered to build the church for him.

Pleased with the offer, the farmer asked how many men would be needed to complete the task. The stranger replied that he would build it himself. Amazed, the farmer then asked what payment the man would expect. The stranger said that if the farmer discovered what his name was before the church was finished, the work would be free. But if the farmer failed to reveal the stranger's name, he must hand over his six year-old son. The farmer agreed to the terms, convinced that he could easily discover the strange man's name.

Day after day and night after night the stranger worked. A man obsessed, he spoke to only a few people and focused on building the church. As if by magic, the building took shape and rose high above its foundation.

The farmer realized that the church would be finished well before the hay-making season was over. He frantically travelled across the countryside asking everyone he met if they knew the name of the strange builder. After weeks of searching he returned home, unsuccessful.

The final day of construction arrived. Grief-stricken, the farmer walked through his field weeping over the great price he would soon pay the builder. He collapsed onto a small grass-covered hill. A few moments later, he thought he heard a voice. Someone was singing. He put his ear to the ground and realized that it was a mother lulling her child to sleep.

Over and over she sang these words:

Soon will your father Finnur,
Bring you a playmate from Reynir,
He's bringing a fine little laddy
Ah, Finnur, your very own daddy.

The farmer immediately guessed who the woman was singing about. He leaped to his feet and ran full speed back to the church. With a heart filled with joy, he entered the building and found the stranger pounding the final nail into a plank above the altar.

"You have finished your work in record time!" said the farmer. "Well done, my friend Finnur!"

No sooner had the word "Finnur" passed the farmer's lips than the stranger vanished and was never seen again.

Based on Jón Árnason I, 57–58

Redhead the Man-Whale

Ancient legend tells us of men risking their lives to hunt for Great Auks in southern Iceland. Men would row their boats far out to sea, far from the mainland, to rocky islands where the black and white seabirds had their breeding ground. The men would hunt during the breeding season, when both birds and eggs are plentiful.

One day, when the weather was calm, a group of men decided to attempt a hunt. When they arrived at an island, most of the men climbed onto the boulders while a few kept watch in the boat.

Suddenly, a great wind arose and the surf buffeted the vessel against the rocks. Fearing for their lives, the men in the boat called for the hunters to return. With great difficulty, the hunters jumped aboard the rocking boat. One young man, hunting high on the rocks, did not hear their cries and was left behind.

Now this young man was the sole support for his widowed mother. When the men returned to shore, they promised her that they would return to rescue her son. They tried all season to get back to the cliffs, but the weather was too severe. When many days had passed, they gave up hope. No man could survive in those harsh conditions for so many days.

Another season came and the group of men again set out for the island. When they landed on the rocks, they were shocked to see the young man walking toward them. He greeted them and asked for passage back to the mainland. They agreed, but wondered how he had survived for so long in such a desolate place. He vaguely answered their questions, saying only that he had passed the time in comfort. Many of the men came to believe that the elves were responsible for his safety.

The following summer, in the community of Hvalsnes, a large number of people were attending a service at the local church. That day, as they filed out of the building, each person passed a magnificent cradle sitting on the porch. A beautiful baby lay inside, covered in a richly embroidered blanket made from the finest fabric. The parishioners peered into the cradle, but none claimed the child as their own.

When the priest came out of the church, he admired the baby and wondered at the beautiful coverlet. "Whose child is this?" he asked. But no one stepped forward to claim it.

As he looked into the faces of the crowd, he spotted the young man who had survived on the rocky island. Suspicious, he called the young man aside and asked, "Do you know who the father of this child is and whether it has been baptized?"

The youth swore he did not know the child or the father. "Why would I care if this child is baptized?" he said. "Christen it or drown it. Whatever you think best. The child, its father, and its mother are nothing to me."

And with those words a beautiful and noble woman, dressed in exquisite clothing, appeared on the porch. Angrily she grabbed the cover from the cradle, threw it into the church and said, "All of you are witnesses. Here is my payment to the church for this child's baptism."

She turned to the young man and said through her

tears, "You faithless coward. Because you disown your own, you will become a fierce and dreaded creature in the sea." And she picked up the cradle with the child in it and vanished.

The priest took the coverlet and placed it on the altar. When people saw it, they said it was the most beautiful altar-cloth ever made.

As for the young man, he immediately went insane and raced toward the cliffs. As he hesitated at the edge, the people saw a great change come over him. He swelled to an enormous size and weight. He became so large that the rock where he stood crumbled and sent him plunging into the sea.

After observing her son's fate, the young man's mother turned to the church crowd and told the rest of his story.

It seems the young man had spent his time on the rocky island in the company of elves. When he realized he was stranded, he despaired of ever being rescued. He thought it would be easier to jump to his death than suffer cold and starvation. The beautiful woman they observed at the church came to his rescue and offered him sanctuary. She told him she was an elf and asked him to spend the winter with her. She became pregnant with their child, but the young man was not content to remain on the island.

Finally she allowed him to return to the mainland with the one condition that when the baby was born, he would have it baptized. He agreed. She told him she would place the child on the church porch at the appointed time. If he failed her, he would be punished.

The old woman went on to say that her son's failure to keep his part of the bargain led to his being turned into a huge whale.

The whale took up residence in the bay of Faxaflói and spent his time haunting the sailors and fishermen. He was easy to recognize because at the time of the elf-woman's curse, he had been wearing a red cap, and now he had a red head. The whale was reported to have killed many men and damaged many vessels, but none were able to kill him or drive him out to sea.

There was also an old priest who lived on Faxaflói bay. He was blind, but healthy and strong. He had two sons and a daughter whom he dearly loved. His sons were fishermen and one day they encountered Redhead. The whale overturned their boat and drowned them both. When their father heard of their fate, he was overcome with grief.

This priest was skilled in the art of magic. Not long after his sons' deaths, he asked his daughter to guide him to the seashore. There he placed his staff into the waves, leaned on it and fell into deep thought.

After a minute he asked his daughter, "What does the sea look like?"

She replied, "It is bright and smooth like a mirror."

A few moments later, the priest asked again, "What does the sea look like?"

She replied, "I see a black line on the horizon. It is moving this way. Perhaps it is a group of whales swimming into the bay?"

When the priest heard this, he asked her to lead him toward the inland side of the bay. As they walked, the black surging sea followed them. As the water became shallow, the girl realized that what she'd thought was a group of whales was in actuality a single, huge, red-headed one. It was rapidly following them, as though drawn by an unseen force, down the middle of the bay.

The priest asked his daughter to lead him up the river that fed into the bay. As they slowly walked along the bank, the whale followed. It was a great struggle for the whale because there was very little water for so great a beast. Yet on they walked until the river became so narrow and the cliffs on each side so high they could feel the earth shake as the whale struggled to follow.

When they reached a waterfall, the whale leaped into the air and landed in the river above. The priest did not stop walking until they reached the lake that fed the river that flowed to the sea. By the time they reached the source of the river, the whale was so exhausted his heart broke under the stress and he sank to the bottom of the lake.

The old priest and his daughter returned home and all the people far and wide thanked them for freeing them from Redhead, the terror of the sea.

And in case you doubt the truth of this story, you should know that mighty whale's bones were found washed ashore on the beaches of Lake Hvalsnes.

Based on Jón Árnason I, 81–82

Hildur, Queen of the Elves

Long ago, in the land where the elves dwell, there lived a girl of common birth. Now it happened that the King of the Elves fell in love with her. His mother was outraged, but the king married her anyway. After the marriage ceremony, the king's mother placed a curse on their union. She said to her son, "This is my curse and it shall be carried out. This fair queen you love shall become a servant in the upper world. You will see her but once a year on Christmas Eve. Each time she visits, there will be a great price to pay."

Far from the land of the elves, in a mountainous region, there lived a farmer whose name we do not know. He was not married, but had a clean and thrifty housekeeper named Hildur. Although she offered no information about her previous life or her family, the farmer trusted her and placed her in charge of his household. The woman was kind and gentle. The farmhands, as well as the farmer himself, were very fond of her.

Unfortunately, this farmer had a problem keeping the shepherds he hired. It was not that he treated the shepherds unkindly, or that the housekeeper failed to provide for their every comfort. The problem was that every Christmas Day morning, one of the the newly hired shepherds would be found dead in his bed. Neither the farmer nor any member of his household was ever suspected of causing these deaths because no wounds were found on the bodies.

Eventually the farmer decided that he could no longer hire shepherds since he knew they were destined for certain death. He would let luck take care of the sheep or the sheep take care of themselves.

One day a determined, strong, and healthy young man offered to shepherd his sheep.

"I will not hire you," the farmer said to the stranger. "I can get along without your help."

The stranger asked, "Have you already hired a shepherd for this winter?"

"No," the farmer replied. "And I will not. Every shepherd I hire ends up dead."

"I heard about that," said the stranger. "But I have no fear of death and I will take good care of your sheep. Please change your mind."

The farmer shook his head in wonder. "It is a pity that so fine a young man is willing to lose his life. Go away. Find work on some other farm."

The stranger repeated over and over that he did not fear the Christmas Eve horror. Eventually the farmer gave in and hired him.

Now in those days it was the custom to spend Christmas Eve in church. Since the farmer's cottage was a great distance away from the fields, the herdsmen did not return with the flocks until very late in the evening. So when the family left for church, Hildur always stayed behind to take care of the house and finish preparing the Christmas Day feast. When the family returned from church and the herdsmen returned from the fields, they always found Hildur busy with her tasks.

On this Christmas Eve, the farmer and his family left for church. Later in the evening the shepherd returned from the flock, ate his supper, and retired for the night. As he snuggled down between the sheets, he remembered what night it was. He recalled the fate of the other shepherds and knew it was important that he stay awake.

As he lay there, he heard the family return from church, enter the house, eat their supper and go to bed. Knowing that he could be in great danger, he struggled to keep his eyes open. Whenever they closed for even a moment, a strange and deadly faintness overcame him. The sensation only increased his determination to stay awake.

Late into the night, the shepherd heard someone quietly approach his bed. He thought it was the housekeeper so he pretended to be asleep. Hildur placed the bit of a magic bridle into the shepherd's mouth. Using the power of the bridle, she dragged the shepherd from his bed and out the cottage door. The shepherd could not resist when Hildur climbed onto his back and made him rise into the air as though he had wings. She rode as fast as she could until they came upon a great cliff that opened up into the very depths of the earth.

Hildur dismounted, fastened the reigns to a stone, and disappeared over the cliff. The shepherd knew he was powerless to follow her as long as the bit remained in his mouth. So he hit his head against the stone and struggled until the bridle fell off.

Even knowing that he might pay for his curiosity with his life, the shepherd leaped over the cliff and sank deep into the darkness. When he reached the bottom, he spotted the housekeeper and followed her to the edge of a beautiful green meadow. Since he could not pursue her across the field without being seen, he took a magic stone, which he happened to carry with him wherever he went, from his pocket. He placed the stone in his left hand and ran after the housekeeper.

In the distance stood a magnificent palace. As Hildur approached the gate, she was greeted by a great crowd. A man, dressed like a king, led them. When the king reached Hildur, he embraced her as a wife and the crowd bowed to her as their queen. Beside the king stood two grown children who, with tears of joy, embraced their mother.

The invisible shepherd followed the crowd into the palace. They gathered in a room that had magnificent hangings on the walls and rows of tables loaded with golden dishes and delicious foods and wines. He found a safe spot to hide where he was out of the way yet could see all the activities.

A short time later, Hildur entered the Great Hall. She was dressed in royal garments and her hands were adorned with golden rings and bracelets. The assembled guests took their seats around the tables and a great feast began. The lords and ladies danced and entertained themselves while the royal couple spoke quietly together. The herdsman saw that they were very much in love and very sad.

While he stood watching, three small children ran into the room and embraced their mother. Hildur returned their embraces with all the love in a mother's heart. She set the youngest of the three on her lap and hugged him close. When he became restless, as most young ones do, she set him on the floor and handed him one of her rings. The boy played with the ring for a short time, but soon lost interest. The shepherd quickly snatched it up and placed it in his pocket. Later on, the guests searched for the ring, but it was nowhere to be found.

As the evening progressed, the shepherd noticed an ugly old woman sitting in the corner. She did not greet the queen with joy nor, when Hildur prepared for her departure, did she raise her voice in protest as the others did.

He watched as the king approached the woman and said, "Take away your curse, Mother. Allow my queen to remain in her home and not be apart from me. These visits are too short. They bring me great joy when she arrives and great pain when she departs."

"Never!" the old woman replied. "My curse stays. I will not change my mind."

When the king saw the hopelessness of his plea, he turned to Hildur, embraced her, and begged her to remain with him.

"Your mother's curse forces me to go," she said. "I am afraid that this may be my final visit. Soon it will be impossible to keep the murders a secret." Smiling through her tears she said, "Once I am discovered, I will face the full penalty for the crimes I have committed against my will."

While the housekeeper was speaking these words, the shepherd ran from the palace, back to where he had entered the darkness. Placing the magic stone into his pocket, he slipped the bridle onto his head and waited for Hildur's return.

When she arrived, she grabbed the bridle and rode the shepherd back to the cottage. Once there, she removed the bridle and gently laid him on his bed. The shepherd knew that it was safe for him to sleep and he did not wake up until late Christmas morning.

The farmer woke up early, his heart filled with fear for the shepherd. He quickly dressed, woke the others in the house, and sneaked up to the shepherd's bed. Gently placing a hand on his chest, the farmer realized that the man was alive. Everyone rejoiced.

When the shepherd finally rose from his slumber, the farmer asked him if anything strange had happened in the night.

"No," he said. "But I had a very strange dream." And he related to his master all the events of the previous night.

When he was finished, Hildur said, "Everything he says is a lie. Before you believe him make him prove by some token that he speaks the truth."

The shepherd reached into his pocket and presented the golden ring. "Here is proof that I was among the elves last night. Is this not your ring, Queen Hildur?"

"The ring is mine," she said. "You are a lucky man. You will prosper in all you do. That is my gift to you."

She recounted her story for all to hear and when she was finished said, "It took a courageous man, willing to follow me into the land of the elves and somehow prove that he was there, to free me from my mother-in-law's curse. I long for my home and my family." And she vanished from their sight, never to be seen again.

As for the shepherd, he married, built a house, and became the most prosperous farmer in the district. People often turned to him for advice and for the rest of his life he gave thanks to Hildur, Queen of the Elves.

Based on Jón Árnason I, 105–109

The Story of Geirlaug

Around the middle of the 7th century, on a poor farm in the Kelda district, there lived two sisters, Sigrídur and Geirlaug. For reasons no one else knows, their mother Ása adored Sigrídur but disliked Geirlaug.

Attending Mass on Christmas Eve was a tradition everyone enjoyed. If the unpredictable winter weather permitted travelling, Ása always insisted that Sigrídur accompany her to church and that Geirlaug stay behind to milk the cows. Ása knew that Geirlaug was frightened to stay home alone, especially on Christmas Eve when the elves came out to celebrate.

Sigrídur and Geirlaug's father dearly loved his daughters and understood Geirlaug's fear. So every year, he found a way for the girls to stay at home together, thus avoiding any possibility that the elves would visit their farm.

The years passed and one day a young man from Laugar began courting Sigrídur. He eventually won her hand in marriage and she happily left her parents' farm and went to live with her new husband.

Geirlaug suspected that on the next Christmas Eve, her mother would again insist that she stay home alone. So at the start of winter, she asked if she could visit her sister. At first Ása refused. But when Geirlaug's father intervened, she gave her permission—on one condition—that Geirlaug be away for no more than one week. Since winter daylight was short, the journey would take two days. Geirlaug would have only three nights to spend with her sister.

Geirlaug happily accepted her mother's demand. In preparation for the long walk over sharp lava and sand, she sewed several pairs of sheepskin shoes. Once she was finished, she set off on her journey.

The two days of travel passed quickly. Geirlaug safely arrived at her sister's farm and received a warm welcome. The sisters enjoyed every moment of their time together, but each of them often mentioned that the visit was far too short.

On her last day, Geirlaug confided to her sister that she was very unhappy at home. Now that Sigrídur was gone, there was no way to avoid staying home alone on Christmas night. She was frightened and begged her sister for help in dealing with the elves when they came to the farm.

Sigrídur agreed and prepared a bundle, filled with flour, lard, and animal fat. She told her sister to hide it from their mother so it wouldn't be taken away. On Christmas night, after everyone was gone, she should make flatbread from the flour, fry it in the lard, and use the rest of the fat to make candles. She should gather some mussel shells, place them around the house, and burn the candles in them. In that way, the entire farm would be bright and well lit. Then she should read the scriptures and sing a few hymns. When she was finished, she should lie down and not worry, no matter what happened later in the night.

Sigrídur gave Geirlaug a pair of new shoes and food for her journey home. The sisters lovingly parted and Geirlaug walked for two days, arriving at the farm just before twilight. She secretly hid her bundle of flour and fat in a place where her mother would never find it.

On Christmas night, as Geirlaug expected, her mother ordered her to stay home alone. After the household left for Mass, Geirlaug did everything her sister suggested. First she placed lighted candles around the farmhouse. Then she sang several hymns and read from the scriptures. She baked the flatbread and while it was still hot, divided it, along with the butter and lard, into three equal portions. She filled three plates with food and placed them on a shelf above her bed. Before retiring for the night, she checked to make sure every candle was burning and that the passageways and rooms were well lighted.

Geirlaug locked up the house and climbed into the bed closest to the entryway of the living room. After a time, she heard thuds and loud noises coming from the front of the house. A few moments later, three handsome young boys raced into the living room and put their chins onto the side of Geirlaug's bed. They stared at her without saying a word. Although she was frightened, Geirlaug reached for the three plates on the shelf above her head and handed them to the boys.

Each boy took a plate and silently ran out of the room. As they disappeared from sight, Geirlaug wondered what would happen when her mother discovered that the plates were missing. To her delight, the boys quickly returned and placed the empty plates at the foot of her bed.

A short time later, Geirlaug again heard noises and voices at the front of the house. A man, who sounded like a leader, said, "This is a well kept home. It is well lit and although few people live here, they are good people."

Geirlaug silently huddled in the corner of the bed, covered by a blanket. She peeked out of a tiny hole and saw a huge crowd of people gathering in the living room. As she watched, the men brought in tables and the women placed expensive foods and delicious drinks onto them.

An elderly man and woman sat at the head table. Geirlaug guessed that they were the leaders of their people. When the glorious banquet was finished, everyone started dancing and playing games. The elderly man sat by the east window and watched the horizon. Every now and then he would say, "Continue playing your games. Day has not yet dawned."

When light began to peek over the mountains, he said, "It is time to stop playing. Dawn has arrived."

At his words, everyone in the room fell silent. Following the elderly man's instructions, the people quickly removed the food from the tables and hauled everything out of the house. The last person left in the room was the elderly woman. She approached Geirlaug's bed and placed a tightly wrapped bundle on her pillow.

"This is a gift for you, Geirlaug my love," she said. "For what you gave to my children. Your mother will try to take this gift away from you, but I promise she will not succeed. The moment she tries, your life will be filled with good luck."

And she followed the others out of the house.

Geirlaug's heart pounded with excitement. She opened the bundle and uncovered a very expensive woolen skirt and a beautifully stitched waistcoat.

Later that morning, Geirlaug's parents returned from the Christmas Mass. Geirlaug told them everything that happened during the night and showed them the beautiful clothes. But she did not mention the kind words of the elf-woman.

When Ása finished examining the clothing, she said, "I do not think the elf-woman meant to give these to you. You are not important enough to wear such beautiful garments. They must be her payment to me for allowing her family to use my house without permission. They are a fitting price for coming into my house uninvited. You will never, ever get to wear them. I will sell them to the priest's wife in Garður. She is a woman who is worthy to wear them."

Geirlaug was too frightened of her mother to object and her father was undecided about what should be done with the garments. So he remained silent and avoided arguing with his wife.

On New Year's Eve the old woman took the clothes to Garður and sold them to the priest's wife. To everyone's surprise, on New Year's Day, the garments disappeared from the priest's house. They reappeared on Geirlaug's bed, wrapped in a bundle that was sitting exactly where the elf-woman had first placed them.

Ása grabbed the clothing from Geirlaug and returned them to the priest's wife. The very next morning, the bundle reappeared on Geirlaug's bed.

That night, Ása had a dream. An angry woman stood by her bed and demanded that she stop taking Geirlaug's clothes. The woman warned that if she didn't stop, she would come to Ása in person and force her to stop. A frightened Ása never touched Geirlaug's clothing again.

A year passed and it was Christmas Eve again. This time, Ása decided that Geirlaug should go to church and she would tend the farm and milk the cows.

Delighted to leave her behind, father and daughter set off for midnight Mass.

Later that night, Ása lit one candle and lay down in Geirlaug's bed. A short time later, she heard voices coming from the front passageway. Three boys raced into the room and rested their chins on the bed, just like they had the year before. Ása became very angry. She demanded to know what they were doing in her house and ordered them to get out and go home.

When the boys didn't obey as fast as she thought they should, Ása grabbed her dirty kitchen dress and whipped it at the side of the bed, hitting each one in the face. With her screaming voice following them, the three boys raced out of the room.

A short while later, Ása heard more noise and voices coming from the front of the house. She watched as a crowd of people entered the living room and set up tables just like they had the previous Christmas Eve. They celebrated throughout the night and when morning came, just like before, they cleaned up the mess and left the house.

But this time, when the elderly woman walked up to Ása's bed, she said, "I need to speak to you about your treatment of my boys."

She grabbed Ása's foot and yanked her off the bed. She pulled so hard that when the old woman landed on the floor, her thigh bones broke. Without a backward glance, the elderly elf-woman followed the rest of her family out of the house.

Ása lay on the floor, paralyzed, until her family returned from Mass. Geirlaug found her mother on the floor and helped her into bed. For the next several weeks, she gently nursed her back to health.

Ása regretted how terribly she had treated her

kind and caring daughter. She was so ashamed of her behavior that from that time on, she became a good and loving mother. But as a reminder of her unkind past, for the rest of her life she stood stooped over and walked with a limp.

Later that winter, Geirlaug met a handsome young man from outside the district. He began courting her and soon asked for her hand in marriage. Geirlaug eagerly accepted his proposal.

Ása asked the young man to move to their farm and in the spring, he did. The young couple was married that summer and took over the running of the farm. Geirlaug's parents lived with her until they died.

Geirlaug and her husband dearly loved each other. They had several children and enjoyed many years together tending their farm. Just like the elf-woman promised, Geirlaug's life was filled with good luck and she became one of the richest and best-loved women in the county.

Based on Jón Árnason III, 170–173

The Elves' Dance on New Year's Eve

Once there were two brothers who constantly argued about whether or not elves really existed. One brother insisted that they did; the other insisted that they did not. Their argument continued for many years and became so intense that the brother who denied the elves' existence became so angry that he decided to leave home. He announced to his family that he would only return when he knew for certain whether or not elves truly lived.

After making this declaration, the man took his dog and travelled over mountains, through the dales and across vast wastelands in search of the elves.

One New Year's Eve, the traveller arrived at a farm. Instead of finding the household gaily celebrating the holiday, he discovered a group of very unhappy people. Curious to know why, he asked what was stopping them from enjoying such a happy occasion.

Their reply surprised the traveller. They were sad because no one could attend midnight Mass. For the past several years, anyone left guarding the farm on New Year's Eve had disappeared while the others were away. Fearing it could happen again, no one ever stayed alone on the farm.

The young traveller laughed at the men for believing in such a silly superstition. Then he offered to guard the farm and prove that there was nothing to fear. The farmer accepted his offer and although he worried about what might happen later that night, he allowed everyone in the household to go to church.

Once he was alone, the traveller set to work. He went into the main room of the house, grabbed a plank from the wall and ripped it off. Then he slid behind the paneling and pulled the plank back into place, leaving a small opening so he could clearly view the entire room.

A few moments later, he heard noises and then footsteps coming into the house. A large number of men and women filtered into the room. Suddenly, to the young man's horror, one of them picked up his dog and flung it to the ground. The dog landed so hard that even behind the paneling, he could hear its bones breaking.

The traveller held his breath when several of the strangers announced that they could smell a human. The others replied that it wasn't unusual since the humans had only recently left for church. Content with that answer, they began setting up tables and covering them with gold embroidered cloth. Onto each table, they placed silver bowls and platters, and beautiful goblets and knives.

Before the visitors sat down to enjoy their splendidly prepared meal, they positioned a small boy in the doorway. He was to keep watch and tell them when dawn arrived. The boy popped in and out of the main room, each time announcing the number of hours left before daybreak.

Whenever the boy left his position, the young man behind the paneling silently loosened some of the framework from around the doorway.

When the banquet was finished, a man and woman walked to the front of the crowd. A third person, who was dressed like a priest, stood with them. The visitors began singing psalms like those sung at a marriage service in a Christian church. As soon as the marriage service was over, laughter filled the room and the floors vibrated from their dancing.

Some time later, the boy-guard reentered the main room. When asked how much of the night remained, he said that there was one watch left. At that same moment, the young traveller slipped out from behind the framework of the door and stood behind the boy. He yelled out, "He's a liar! Daylight is filling the sky!" and then quickly slipped back behind the framework, into the wall, and out of sight.

The elves were so upset by that announcement that they killed the small boy. In a panic, they raced out of the house, leaving all their possessions behind.

The young traveller jumped out of the wall and chased after them. He followed the elves to a lake that lay near the farm. To his amazement, one by one the elves flung themselves into the water. When the last water-elf disappeared beneath the surface, the traveller returned to the farm and gathered up the leftover food and valuable dishes.

Shortly after dawn, the household returned from church. They joyfully greeted the young man and asked if anything unusual had happened during the night. He told them the entire story. Apparently the other men who were left to guard the farm must have been seen by the elves. And just like his dog, that mistake had cost them their lives.

The entire household thanked the young man for his services and rewarded him with as many of the elves' valuables as he could carry.

The young man returned to his home. He told his family about his adventures and said that he would never again deny the existence of elves.

Years later, he married, inherited his parent's farm, and lived a long and prosperous life.

And if you are wondering what happened at the farm where he spied on the elves, it is said that no man ever disappeared from there again.

Based on Jón Árnason I, 117–118

TWO

Trolls

Blessing the Cliffs

For centuries, men have hunted birds and collected their eggs from the cliffs that surround Iceland. Since the early 12th century, legends tell of how priests blessed those cliffs, trying to force the trolls who live there to flee. Here are a few of their stories.

The first story is attributed to Bishop Thorlákur the Saint, who died in 1193. One day he was asked to bless the cliffs of Látrabjarg in the west of the country. As sea birds circled overhead, he slowly walked along the edge, blessing each area and driving out the evil spirits.

Suddenly, a voice rose up from the rocks below his feet. "Even the wicked must have a place to live," the troll said.

Thorlákur sympathized with the troll's plight and left a small area unblessed. He warned the people from the nearby parish never to drop a rope from that spot. No one dared disobey him until the day a foolish man decided it was the perfect place to hunt. He lowered a rope and climbed down. As he grasped the first bird egg, a gray hand reached out from inside the rock and cut his rope. The man tumbled to his death.

A second story is attributed to Bishop Gudmundur the Good, who died in 1237. This legend insists that he was the first to bless those same cliffs, but Bishop Thorlákur the Saint might have argued that point.

Gudmundur was wandering homeless around the west of the country when he happened upon the cliffs of Látrabjarg and decided to bless them. When he was almost finished, a voice called out from inside the rock, "Bishop, I beg you. Stop your prayers and ceremonies. We will be forced to flee our home. Even the wicked must have a place to live."

The bishop immediately stopped what he was doing and left an area of the cliffs unblessed. From that time on, whenever he blessed a cliff, he left room for the trolls to live undisturbed.

Another story comes from the early 14th century in a collection of miracles recorded by Bishop Gudmundur Arason the Good.

A man named Eiríkur Árnason was out gathering eggs on a cliff. Since it was dangerous to hunt in the early morning or the late afternoon, he diligently worked throughout the day. Unfortunately, he lost track of time and as the sun began to set, he frantically began climbing back up the face of the cliff.

Suddenly, a hand reached out from the rock and began cutting through his rope. The troll cut eight strands, but the ninth, which had been blessed by Bishop Gudmundur, held strong and saved Eiríkur's life.

Whether or not these stories are true, we know that many of Iceland's cliffs were blessed by bishops. Many bishops pitied the trolls and left a section unblessed so there was a place of sanctuary. To this day, the areas of the cliffs where trolls safely live are called Heidnaberg or the Heathen Cliffs.

Based mainly on Jón Árnason I, 137–138

Gilitrutt

At the time of this story, an energetic, hard-working young farmer had unknowingly married a lazy young woman. Much to his dismay, she idled her days away, never lifting a finger to help. Her behavior irritated the farmer, but there was nothing he could do about it.

The couple's farm sat at the foot of Eyjafjöll on a piece of land that was perfect for grazing a large number of sheep. One autumn day the farmer brought his wife a huge pile of wool and told her to spend the winter weaving it into cloth. Days passed and then weeks, but the woman never touched the wool. Her husband kept reminding her of her duty, but she refused to listen.

One day, an enormous old woman came to the farm begging for alms. The farmer's wife greeted her at the door and said, "Would you do some work for me in return for the charity I give to you?"

"Yes," the old woman replied. "What would you like me to do?"

"I want you to weave some wool into cloth," she said.

"Agreed," said the old woman. "Give me the wool."

The farmer's wife pushed an immensely large bag of wool toward the doorway. She stared in amazement as the old woman grabbed the bag and slung it over her shoulder while saying, "I'll return with the cloth on the first day of summer."

"That is a lot of wool," the wife said. "What additional payment will you expect?"

"Not much," said the old woman. "If you can tell me my name within three guesses, I will be content and ask for no further payment."

The farmer's wife agreed to the terms and the old woman left.

The winter months passed quickly and several times the farmer asked his wife how she was doing with her weaving. She angrily told him that it was no concern of his and he would see the cloth on the first day of summer. The farmer was not pleased with his wife's answer and wondered what she was hiding.

When spring was well on its way, the farmer's wife started thinking about the old woman's name. Realizing that she had no way to discover it, her anxiety grew and she became rude and unhappy. The farmer noticed her distress and asked what was bothering her. In despair, she told him the entire story.

As he listened to her tale, the farmer grew frightened. He realized that the creature who appeared at their door was not really an old woman but a troll. If his wife did not discover her name, she would be snatched up and taken away.

The first day of summer drew near. One morning the farmer took a long walk along the foot of the mountain, trying to think of a way to help his wife. When he passed a large pile of rocks near the entrance to a cave, he heard the sound hammering. Someone was living inside the mountain! He followed the noise and sneaked closer to the cave. Peeking through a small hole, he saw a huge old woman with a loom clasped between her legs. As she weaved, she merrily struck the cloth and sang:

Hi, hi, and ho, ho!
The housewife far below
My name she does not know—
Hi, hi, and ho, ho!
My name is Gilitrutt, you know—
Hi, hi and ho, ho!

The farmer was delighted. Surely this was the same old woman who had visited his farm the past autumn. He returned home, wrote the name Gilitrutt on a piece of paper and tucked it in a safe spot. Hoping to teach his wife a lesson, he decided not to tell her that he had discovered the troll's name.

The last day of winter finally arrived and the farmer's wife was beside herself with worry. She spent the day weeping and refused to even get dressed. The farmer finally took pity on her and asked if she had discovered the old woman's name. She replied that she had not and now she was sure to die from grief and worry. Her husband smiled and said that dying would not be necessary. He handed her the piece of paper with the name written on it and told her how he had discovered it.

Although her heart swelled with hope, the farmer's wife still worried that the name might be wrong. She continued to shake with fright and begged her husband to stay with her when she confronted the old woman.

"You gave her the wool on your own," he said. "It is proper that you pay her alone." And he left the house.

The first day of summer dawned and the farmer's wife was alone in the house. She lay prostrate with fear on her bed. Suddenly, thunderous footsteps approached the front door. The old woman walked straight into the house and threw the bolts of cloth onto the floor. With a very unpleasant look on her face, she demanded, "What is my name? Tell me right now, what is my name?"

Trembling, the young wife said, "Is it Sign??"

"It could be that. It could be that—but it's not! Guess again, Mistress."

"Is it Asa?" asked the wife.

"It could be that. It could be that—but it's not! Guess again, Mistress."

The young wife sat up and said, "I don't suppose your name is Gilitrutt?"

At the sound of her name, the old troll fell flat on her face onto the floor with a gigantic crash. Then, she jumped up, ran out of the house, and was never seen again.

Relieved, the farmer's wife danced with joy. But you can be sure that her narrow escape from the troll completely changed her attitude toward work. From that day on, she worked hard and became an excellent housekeeper. And to the delight of her husband, she always wove her own wool.

Based on Jón Árnason I, 172–173

Gellivör

This story takes place at the end of the Roman Catholic times in Iceland.

On the farm of Hvoll, on a firth in the eastern part of the country, there lived a farmer and his wife. They were quite wealthy and owned huge herds of sheep and cattle. A female troll also lived in the area, on the south side of the firth. But she was a mild-mannered troll and never caused any mischief.

One Christmas Eve, long after dark, the farmer walked out of the farmhouse and disappeared. The entire household searched for him, but he was never found.

Following this disappearance, one of the servants took over the management of the farm. Unfortunately, after dark on the following Christmas Eve, he too disappeared without a trace.

After the second disappearance, the grieving widow decided to remove all of her belongings from the house and spend the rest of the winter somewhere else. She left her sheep and cattle in the care of her shepherds and did not return until the following summer.

As the winter before the third Christmas season approached, the farmer's widow again prepared to leave Hvoll. Promising to return in the spring, she ordered her herdsmen to care for the animals and feed them throughout the winter.

The widow's household was supplied with milk, butter, and cheese from four cows kept in a nearby pasture. One of those cows had given birth to a calf and was producing plenty of creamy milk. Two days before her planned departure, a woman appeared to the widow in a dream. She was dressed in ragged, old fashioned clothes and said to her, "Your cow has just calved, and I have no milk to feed my children. Would you set aside a portion of yours so my children may eat? Please fill a jug and place it on the dairy shelf.

"I know that you plan to leave the farm in two days' time. You fear living here through the winter because you do not know what happened to your husband and your servant on the last two Christmas Eves. I must tell you that a female troll lives in the nearby mountain. She is mild tempered, but two years ago she had a child with a strange appetite and disposition. Her child demands human flesh and she is forced to provide it each Christmas. If you are willing to supply me with milk, I will advise you on how to banish the troll."

The moment she said her last word, the woman disappeared.

The widow woke and remembered her dream. She rose from her bed, entered the dairy, filled a wooden jug with fresh milk and placed it in the designated spot. No sooner had the jug settled onto the shelf, than it disappeared. The next evening, the widow returned to the dairy and found an empty jug. She refilled it with milk, set it down, and smiled as it again vanished from sight.

Deciding to trust the woman, the widow remained on the farm. Each morning she filled a jug with milk and counted the days until the Christmas season.

When Christmas Eve finally arrived, the widow and the woman again met in a dream. The woman greeted her and said, "You are not a very inquisitive person.

You never asked who received your daily supply of milk. But I will tell you anyway. I am an elf-woman and I live in the little hill near your house. You have treated me kindly all through the winter, but I no longer need your milk. Yesterday, my cow had a calf and she has plenty of it to spare. As a reward for your kindness, I have placed a small gift on the shelf in the dairy.

"I also want to save you from the troll. At midnight, you will wake up and feel an overwhelming urge to go outside. Don't resist. When you pass through the doorway, you will come face to face with the troll. She will wrap her arms around you and carry you across a grassy field, over a river and toward the mountain where she lives. When you get to the far side of the river, cry out, 'What is that sound?' and she will immediately ask you, 'What did you hear?'

"Your answer must be, 'I heard someone cry, Mamma Gellivör, Mamma Gellivör!'

"She will think this strange because no human knows her name. Her reply will be, 'Oh, I suppose it is that naughty child of mine.' And she will put you down and run up the mountain.

"In the meantime, while she is distracted with you, I will go to her cave and mercilessly thump and pinch her child. As soon as she is out of sight, turn your back on the mountain and run as fast as you can to the nearest farm along the riverbank.

"When the troll returns and overtakes you, she will say, 'Why did you move, you wretch?' and she will again take you in her arms and turn toward the mountain.

"As soon as you have gone a short way, cry out again, 'What is that sound?'

"She will ask again, 'What did you hear?'

"You must reply, 'I thought I heard someone calling, 'Mamma Gellivör, Mamma Gellivör!'

"She will drop you to the ground and run toward the mountain. You must dash to the nearest church, making sure you arrive before her return. If she overtakes you and snatches you up, she will treat you horribly. She will be overwhelmed with grief and anger because I pinched and thumped her child to death. But if you fail to reach the church, don't be afraid—I will be there to help you."

The widow woke from her dream, climbed out of bed, and went to the dairy. Lying on the milk shelf was a large bundle and tucked inside were an intricately embroidered dress, belt, and cap.

When midnight arrived and everyone on the Hvoll farm was asleep, the widow felt an overwhelming urge to go outside. As she passed over the threshold to the house, she was immediately seized and lifted high into the air. She was crushed in the arms of a gigantic troll and quickly carried over the river and toward the mountain.

Everything happened exactly as the elf-woman foretold, until the troll flung the widow down for the second time. As she ran toward the church, she felt someone grip her arms, lifting her up and helping her along. When the rumble from a tremendous landslide on the mountain shook the ground, the widow looked over her shoulder. She watched in horror as the troll furiously stomped through a spongy swamp in her direction. At the sight of the troll, the widow almost fainted. It was then that the unseen someone lifted her off the ground and sailed toward the church. The widow was shoved through the sanctuary doors, and they were immediately slammed shut behind her.

Inside the sanctuary, a crowd of people had gathered for worship and were celebrating early Mass. As soon as the widow passed through the door, the church bells rang out and everyone in the building felt the impact of something heavy falling to the ground. When they peered out of a window, the people saw a huge troll scurrying away. Apparently the troll was so frightened by the sound of the bells that in her haste, she stumbled and knocked down a portion of the wall that surrounded the churchyard.

Staring at the fallen wall, the troll cursed it and said, "Never stand again!"

A short time later, the troll abandoned her cave and settled on a mountain far away from the parish of Hvoll.

Another story about Gellivör happened on Bláskógár Mountain in the south of the country. For two years she haunted the passes, becoming so mischievous that few people even attempted to cross the mountain.

This particular year, the inhabitants of Thinge-yarsysla discovered that their calculation of dates was incorrect and they didn't know the exact day for Christmas. In an attempt to fix the error, the villagers decided to send a message to the bishop in the village of Skálholt, asking him for help. They agreed to send a bold and youthful man named Ólafur across the mountain to deliver their request.

Ólafur set off on his journey and late in the day was passing over Bláskógár Mountain. Not wanting to face the troll, he hurried along as quickly as possible.

At twilight, Gellivör appeared in his path and said, "Are you going south, Ólafur? I gladly warn you to go home. Return with shame to your own place."

Ólafur replied, "Oh, troll on the mountain, greetings! I hope you are well."

Surprised by his words, she said, "Over the years, few have greeted me so kindly. You are a dear man. Pass safely." And she let him continue on his way without eating him.

Ólafur arrived in Skálholt and contacted the bishop. He delivered his message and in return received the exact day for Christmas.

On his way home, he again passed over the mountain. He encountered Gellivör, but this time she seemed far less threatening. When he approached her, she offered him a book. It was a troll-almanac or calendar.

As she handed it to him, she said, "If the Christ, son of Mary, had done as much for trolls as he did for humans, we would never be so ungrateful as to forget the date of his birth."

Ólafur, who was not a very gracious man, said to her, "Look! To the east. Who is it that rides on a white horse?"

The troll turned to look and at that moment, dawn broke over the mountain and she was turned to stone.

Based on Jón Árnason I, 148–151

Katla and the Magic Shoes

This story happened at the monastery at Thykkvabær after the Abbot hired a housekeeper named Katla. Katla managed to frighten everyone— even the Abbot himself. She was mean-spirited and bad-tempered; she mercilessly berated everyone. Usually her ranting and raving was aimed at Bardi, the monastery's herdsman. And she was especially vicious if he lost one of their sheep.

Katla owned a unique pair of shoes. Anyone who wore them could run long distances and never grow tired.

One fine autumn day, Katla and the Abbot decided to attend a wedding. Before she left the farm, Katla ordered Bardi to bring in the sheep and milk the ewes. She told him that she wanted the job finished by the time she returned home. Unfortunately, when Bardi rounded up the flock, several of the ewes were missing. In an attempt to avoid Katla's anger, he ran into the house and grabbed her magic shoes. After placing them on his feet, he jumped up and dashed out the door.

Bardi searched everywhere. He travelled great distances until finally, he found the missing animals. Since the shoes protected him from feeling any fatigue, he rounded up the ewes, herded them back to the flock, and then quickly moved the flock to the farm.

When Katla returned home, she immediately knew that Bardi had used her shoes. Blinded by anger, she grabbed him and drowned him in a vat of cheese curds.

Many people at the monastery wondered what happened to the shepherd, but no one suspected that Katla was involved in his disappearance.

As winter progressed, the curds in the tub sank lower and lower.

One day, Katla was heard muttering, "Soon ripples in the milk will reveal the soles of Bardi's feet!"

Katla feared that Bardi's murder would be discovered. She knew that she would be accused of the crime and condemned to death. So, shortly after she muttered those words, Katla put on her magic shoes and ran away from the monastery. She raced up the icy mountain, leaped into a rift and disappeared from sight. No one ever saw Katla again.

The moment she sailed over the edge of the rift, the mountain erupted. The earth shook and lava spewed out, flowing swiftly down into the valley, enveloping the monastery.

Many of the people who survived said that Katla's witchcraft caused the eruption. From that day, the crater in the mountain has been called the Rift of Katla.

Based on Jón Árnason I, 175–176

Trunt, Trunt and the Trolls in the Fells

One time two men walked up a mountain to gather herbs. As evening approached, they pitched their tent and settled in for the night. One of the men immediately fell asleep, but the other lay wide awake.

Suddenly, the sleeping man sat up and crawled out of the tent. His friend followed, anxious to know where he was going. Once outside, the sleeping man took off at a dead run toward the glaciers. The other man followed, but was barely able to keep up.

With lungs that were ready to burst, the friend stopped his pursuit and struggled to catch his breath. Looking toward the glacier, he spotted a giant she-troll sitting high on a peak. Her arms were outstretched, beckoning the sleeping man to her. Using her magic, the troll charmed the man into running straight into her arms. She lifted him off the ground and walked away.

A year later, people from the district began gathering herbs in the same place. A man came to meet them. He was quiet and sullen, scarcely muttering a word. When they asked him whom he believed in, he replied, "I believe in God."

The next year, the man appeared again. The herb gatherers were amazed to see the change in him. He now appeared more like a troll than a human. Although many were frightened, they asked if he still believed in God. He didn't reply, and this time he remained with them for only a few minutes.

The third year, the man appeared again. By this time, he had changed even more. He was now a fearsome, ugly troll. One brave herb gatherer asked him again if he believed in God.

The troll replied, "I believe in Trunt, trunt and the trolls of the fells."

After saying these words, he disappeared and was never seen again. For many years, no one dared gather herbs in that place.

Based on Jón Árnason I, 183–184

How Kráka Lost Her Lover

In the old days, an evil and destructive troll named Kráka lived in a cave near Bláfjöll Mountain. Perched on a steep and rugged cliff, the cave was impossible for any man to reach. Kráka detested most humans and killed many of the men she encountered. When she wasn't hunting people, she enjoyed capturing and eating cattle that grazed near the village of Mývatn.

Now Kráka had one weakness: she hated to live alone. Whenever loneliness overwhelmed her, she would sneak into the village and kidnap a man from his house. She would haul him to her cave and do anything to try and make him love her. The men seldom responded to her lovemaking, though, and most of them either ran away or killed themselves.

One day, Kráka sneaked onto the Baldursheimur farm near the village of Mývatn at the foot of the mountain. She grabbed a young shepherd named Jón and carried him back to her cave. Once there, she presented him with a magnificent feast. Jón refused her offering and would not eat a single bite. Kráka tried every trick she had learned over the years to please him, but none of them worked.

Eventually Jón grew tired of her attempts to make him happy. Hoping to divert her attention, he gave her what he thought was an impossible task: find a twelve-year-old shark and he would gladly eat it.

Using her magic, Kráka discovered that the only

place to find that shark was at Siglunes, more than seventy miles away. Determined to please her captive and hopeful that obtaining the shark would compel Jón to love her, Kráka decided to make the long journey and catch the fish.

So off she went, leaving the shepherd alone in her cave. After travelling a short distance, Kráka began to wonder if Jón was tricking her. She decided to turn back and see if he was attempting an escape. She ran back to the cave, only to find Jón sitting quietly, patiently waiting for her return.

Off she went again, this time travelling further from the cave. Suddenly, she was gripped with fear. Was Jón being unfaithful to her? Was he trying to escape? She quickly returned to the cave and found him sitting quietly just like before.

Again, she set off on her journey. When images of Jón trying to escape filled her thoughts, she told herself that she could trust him.

To reach Siglunes, Kráka travelled across Bláfjöll Mountain and waded through the widest part of Eyjafjördur just north of Hrísey Island. Once there, she quickly caught the shark and, following the same path, returned to her cave.

Back at the cave, Jón patiently waited until he was sure Kráka would not return. He found a way to escape from his prison and ran as fast as he could toward the Baldursheimur farm.

When Kráka arrived back at the cave, she discovered that Jón was gone. She dropped the shark and set off in hot pursuit.

When Jón heard the pounding thunder of footsteps and the crack of falling trees, he knew that it was Kráka. He could sense her fury. With fear giving him strength, he ran even faster.

As Kráka approached Jón, she called out, "Jón! Here is the shark you wanted. It is not just twelve years old, it is thirteen!"

Jón took no notice of her words and kept on running. He dashed across the farmyard and blindly ran toward the blacksmith shop. Finding the farmer inside, Jón hid behind him at the same moment Kráka reached the doorway. Immediately, the farmer snatched up a bunch of red hot irons from the fire pit and pointed them at the troll. With the irons aimed at her heart, the farmer demanded that she turn around, go home, and promise to never bother him or his men again.

Kráka realized that she had little choice but to leave, and she did. From that moment on, she never bothered the farmer or his household again.

Based on Jón Árnason I, 178–180

The Giantess's Staff

The supernatural beings who live inside the rocks and mountains of Iceland, were miserable when Christianity began to spread throughout the land. And they grew sadder as each new church sprang up.

When a night troll (a giantess, in fact) who lived in Vatnsdalur Mountain heard that the villagers had decided to build a church in nearby Thingeyrar, she was furious. Such disrespect! So near where she lived!

After the church was complete, she decided to take her revenge. She travelled north, to the furthest edge of the mountain, to a place called Öxl. When she arrived, she tightly gripped her staff and then took aim, throwing it directly at the Thingeyrar church, hoping to smash it to the ground.

The moment the staff left her hand, the night troll turned to search the eastern sky. She needed enough time to safely hide from the morning light. Unfortunately, at that very moment, the sun peeked over the mountain and, just like it would for any night troll, sent her tumbling headfirst over the cliffs. She fell down the western side of the mountain and landed on a ledge, a mere stone's throw from the foot of the bluff.

Immediately, her body turned to stone. Today, that night-troll stone sits in the same spot, in a place now called Kerling.

As for the staff, it broke into two pieces as it hurtled through the air. The first piece came down close to the church, in the middle of a paved path that ran along the south side of the building. That portion of the staff was about three yards long and where it impaled the ground was no more than forty yards from the church. Until some time in 1832, the broken staff was used to tie up horses.

The second, shorter portion of the staff landed to the south of the main field at the Thingeyrar farm. As you ride up to the farm, look to the right and you will see that the farmer uses it as part of the corner of his fence.

Based on Jón Árnason I, 208

Grýla

No collection of troll legends would be complete without mentioning Grýla. She is listed among the she-trolls in Snorri Sturluson's work, *Edda*. *Edda* was written in about 1200 and its author was a popular Icelandic poet and politician. This frightening troll also appeared in rhymes and jingles in medieval times.

Grýla was like every other troll. She loved to eat humans and was especially fond of attacking children and full grown men. For centuries parents used stories about Grýla to terrify their children into good behavior.

Early in her history, Grýla was seen as a monster. She was described as having 300 heads with six eyes in each head and two ghostly blue eyes at the back of each neck. She had horns like a goat and her ears were so long that they hung down to her shoulders. On each forehead grew a tuft of hair and on each chin, a tangled, filthy, straggly beard. Her teeth looked like burned lava, her feet were like horse's hoofs, her fingernails were deformed, and she had fifteen tails.

In one rhyme she is described:

> Grýla rode into the yard;
> Fifteen tails had she,
> And on each tail a hundred bags,
> And twenty children in each bag.

And another:

Grýla rode into the yard;
Hoofs she had to walk upon,
From her brow the long tufts hung;
A bag she bore against her thigh—
The children are in there, thought I.

Grýla used her many eyes to spy on human children. And every time she found a naughty child, she grabbed him or her and stuffed them into a big gray sack.

Grýla's husband was Leppalúdi and they had twenty children of their own. She also had thirteen sons from before her marriage. These thirteen sons, who were later linked to the Christmas season and called the Yuletide or Christmas Lads, had delightful names that described their dominant behaviors: Pot Licker, Sausage Snatcher, and Fat Gobbler.

Like their parents Grýla and Leppalúdi, the Yuletide Lads were also very useful for frightening children into good behavior. They came down from the mountains, one at a time, over the thirteen days before Christmas, with the last one arriving on Christmas Eve. They entered the village and were very willing to carry off any child who cried too much or was unruly. Then, on Christmas Day, the first lad would leave the village. One by one they returned to the mountain until the last lad left on the Twelfth Night.

Stories of Grýla began to disappear when styles of parenting changed, and the people of Iceland decided to stop frightening their growing children. Belief in Grýla was abandoned, but the noun *Grýla* (growler) is used to describe a she-troll or a scary boogie man and the verb *ad Grýla* means "to threaten."

However, there is an interesting legend about the Yuletide Lads.

In the east of Iceland, on the Thrúduvangur farm, there lived a farmer named Steinn and his wife Gudrún. In those days, the Christian faith was in its infancy. Steinn himself was not a religious man. Though his wife was a godly woman and regularly attended the parish church, he refused to go with her.

One Christmas Eve, Gudrún asked her husband to accompany her to Vespers, an annual tradition. The night was dark and none of the other men in the household were free to accompany her. Steinn greeted her request with impatience. In the end, however, he agreed to escort her but refused to attend the service.

Steinn, Gudrún, and their son Illugi set off on their journey. When they reached the boundary of the parish, they parted ways, with Steinn returning to the farm and his wife and son continuing on to the church.

The following day, when Gudrún and Illugi returned home, they found Steinn lying in his bed. Gudrún watched over him, but he never moved. Since her husband had never acted like this before, she asked him if he was ill.

"No," he said. "But I don't think I would have returned to the farm so quickly yesterday evening if I knew then what I know now."

Gudrún thought his words were strange, but could not convince him to share his experiences from the night before.

Months passed, and then a year, and the next Christmas season was upon them. On Christmas Eve, Gudrún again asked her husband to accompany her to church. The weather was wild and deep drifts of snow covered the pathways. He agreed to go with them, but he was very quiet during the journey. When they reached the parish boundary, he begged his son to return home with him.

"You will live to see many Christmas seasons," he said to Illugi. "But my life will soon be over. I want you to see what I have seen and benefit from it."

Frightened by his words, Illugi followed his father into the cold winter night. When they reached the storehouse at the edge of their farm, the two men walked inside the building and stood, waiting.

Suddenly, the end wall of the shed slid aside and Illugi could see far to the east. Two men, dressed in white, slowly walked toward them, carrying a coffin with a cloth draped over it. The men stepped into the store-house and stopped in front of Steinn. A multitude of spirits crowded around the coffin, swooping in from every direction and greeting each other. All through the night, the spirits spoke about the women and men, both good and bad, from the parish. But they especially enjoyed talking about naughty children.

After listening to their words, Illugi realized that evil and ungodly men delighted them and that they hated religion and any godly practices.

When the spirits finally spoke to Steinn, they told him that by the next Christmas they would carry him away in their coffin.

Illugi felt the cold of a winter wind emanating from these spirits and he didn't like what he saw. Suddenly, there was a powerful crashing sound and the shed went from light to pitch darkness. Illugi was so frightened, he fainted. When he recovered, he was in his own bed, where his father had carried him.

A short while later, Steinn was dead. Illugi told everyone about what he had seen and heard in the storehouse. They told him that the spirits he saw were the Yuletide Lads. Much like their mother Grýla, they travel throughout the countryside at Christmas, making mischief, and stealing or playing tricks on the children.

As his father had hoped, Illugi learned from what he had witnessed. He lived to a nice old age, attended church regularly, and was confirmed in his faith. He never saw the Yuletide Lads again nor did they do him or his mother any harm.

In fact, they seldom appear and when they do, it is only to the ungodly. Icelanders know that it is a horrible thing to end up in the coffin of the Yuletide Lads!

Based on Jón Árnason I, 121–122, 207–208,

THREE

Ghosts

Mother Mine Don't Weep, Weep

There once was a young servant girl who discovered that she was pregnant. She carried the baby to term and gave birth in secret. Following the delivery, she carried the infant outdoors and laid it, unprotected, onto the cold hard ground. After the child died, she wrapped the body in rags and buried it under the wall of a nearby sheep shed.

It is important to remember that in those days, killing a newborn baby was a sad reality of life for any unmarried girl. The laws in Iceland were so strict that if she didn't, she would face severe punishment and possibly death herself.

A short time after her child's death, the girl received an invitation to a *vikivaki* dance. Such communal dances often occurred around the Christmas and New Year's celebrations and were very popular with people of all ages. These parties could last for days while the guests feasted on delicious foods and spent hours singing and dancing.

The invitation frustrated the servant girl. She desperately wanted to go, but didn't own a dress fancy enough or expensive enough for such an important occasion. Forced to decline the invitation, she stayed home and lamented missing all the fun.

One day, while the dance was going on, the servant girl walked to the sheep shed to help milk the ewes. She joined several other women and they passed the time chatting among themselves.

When the servant girl began to complain about missing the dance because she had nothing to wear, a voice rang out from beneath the pasture wall.

The voice said,

> Mother mine, don't weep, weep,
> As you milk the sheep, sheep;
> I can lend my rags to you,
> So you can go a-dancing too,
> You can go a-dancing too.

The girl knew that this was a message from her dead child. The child's voice and song affected her so deeply that she was never again in her right mind.

Based on Jón Árnason I, 217–218

White Cap

One time, on a farm near a church, there lived a young boy and a young girl. The boy's favorite pastime was finding new and interesting ways to frighten the girl. He persisted to the point where the girl became immune to his behavior and nothing ever frightened her. Whenever something strange or unusual happened, she attributed it to the boy's mischief-making.

One washing day, the girl's mother sent her to the churchyard to fetch some linen that had been laid out to dry. After filling her basket, she looked up and noticed a strange figure sitting on a tombstone in the graveyard. The figure was dressed in white from head to toe.

Thinking that the boy was playing a trick on her again, she was not alarmed. Instead, she ran up to the figure and grabbed the white cap from off its head. "You will not frighten me this time!" she said.

The girl turned away from the figure, collected the rest of her linens and returned home. To her amazement, the boy greeted her the moment she entered the cottage. She was puzzled. It would have been impossible for him to reach the cottage before she did and certainly not without her seeing him. How had he done it?

While sorting the linen, the girl discovered the white cap that she had grabbed from the graveyard figure. It was moldy and filled with dirt. Obviously, it did not belong to anyone in her household.

The next morning, the girl noticed that the figure was still sitting on the same tombstone, minus a cap on its head. Realizing that it was a ghost, she asked everyone in the household if they knew how to talk to it or how to get rid of it. Finding no one to help, a message was quickly sent to the nearby village asking for advice.

An old man answered their query and said that to avoid a great calamity, the young girl must replace the cap on the ghost's head. Since she had taken it, she was obliged to return it. Also, many people must witness the return and remain completely silent until she had restored the cap to its rightful place.

A crowd of villagers gathered at the graveyard to witness the return of the white cap. The frightened girl walked forward, cap in her hand, and placed it gently onto the ghost's head. She said to the ghost, "Are you satisfied now?"

At that moment, the girl fell down dead. As for the ghost, it sank into the grave that it was sitting on and was never seen again.

Based on Jón Árnason I, 231

Lost My Lusty Complexion

One day, a pastor's servant girl approached a country churchyard where several men were digging a grave. At the moment she walked past, the gravediggers turned up an ancient bone. It was a human thigh bone and unusually long.

The light-hearted young woman saw the bone and picked it up. She turned it over in her hands and said, "What fun it would have been to kiss this big man when he was alive!" With a laugh, she placed the bone on the ground and continued on her way.

The day passed quickly. Darkness fell, and all the lamps in the house were lit. Later in the evening, the pastor realized that he needed a book that he had left on the church altar. Knowing that the servant girl was not afraid of the dark, he called for her and asked her to fetch the volume for him.

The girl was very willing to go and quickly left the cottage. She entered the church, walked down the aisle and found the requested book sitting on the altar. When she began to make her way back up the aisle, she noticed that a strange man was sitting near the door. He had a long beard and a body that was so gigantic it filled the corner bench on the north side of the church.

The stranger spoke to the girl:

I lost my lusty complexion,
Curious maiden, see how it's faded;
I was but a lad, whom death laid low,

Lady, behold my cold lids.
My armor was hacked into pieces
Long ago, when I fought in battle;
My whiskers are grown and grimy,
Kiss me, sweet one, if you will.

The girl was not disturbed by the sight of this strange looking man. She sauntered over to him and firmly planted a kiss on his face. She then carried the book back to the house, gave it to the pastor and never told anyone about her encounter.

But there is an alternate ending to this story. It says that when the girl was challenged by the ghost to kiss him, she was so horrified that she ran out of the church and was never seen again.

In any case, everyone agrees that the thigh bone must have come from the grave of a giant man who lived in ancient times. This man's ghost recited the verse to the servant girl and he was the one she saw that night in the church.

Based on Jón Árnason I, 233–234

The Deacon of Myrká

Now it happened in days of old there lived a deacon from the church at Myrká. He loved a serving maid named Gudrún who lived on a farm on the opposite side of the valley. The great Hörgá River separated the betrothed couple.

The deacon had a horse named Faxi who had a long gray mane. Shortly before Christmas, the deacon rode Faxi across the frozen river to the farm where Gudrún lived. He wanted to ask her to accompany him to the Christmas festivities at Myrká and promised to return for her on Christmas Eve.

Now, before his journey across the river, there had been a deep freeze and a heavy snowstorm. The river was covered in ice and the deacon crossed it without incident. But on his return journey, the ice had thawed a bit and was beginning to break up. When the deacon reached the river, he realized that the floating ice and floodwaters would keep him from crossing. He travelled up the banks of the river until he came to an ice bridge. He urged Faxi onto the ice. When they reached the middle of the river, the ice broke beneath the weight of the deacon and the horse, and they plunged into the icy waters.

The next morning, a farmer noticed the deacon's horse grazing in his field, saddle and bridle still on him. Wondering what had happened to the rider, the farmer combed the riverbanks. Eventually he found the deacon's body at a place called Thúfnavellir Point. The floating ice had torn the flesh off the back of the deacon's head and his bare white skull was clearly visible. The farmer brought the body back to Myrká and it was buried during the week before Christmas.

The constantly changing weather kept news from travelling across the river and Gudrún never received word of her beloved's death. On Christmas Eve, Gudrún dressed in her best clothes and eagerly awaited the deacon's arrival.

Later that evening there was a knock on the door. A young woman, who was with Gudrún, answered it, but found no one there. Thinking that darkness was the cause, she said, "Wait, and I will bring a light."

When she closed the door, the visitor knocked again. Thinking it must be the deacon, Gudrún hurried across the room. Slipping one arm into the sleeve of her riding cloak and flinging the rest over her shoulders, she said, "Somebody is playing a trick on us. I will go outside and see for myself."

When she opened the door, Gudrún saw Faxi and a man she thought was the deacon. Without a word the man lifted Gudrún onto his horse and climbed on in front of her. Neither spoke as they rode toward the river. When they reached the bank, Gudrún saw that ice covered all the water except a rapid black stream flowing down the middle. Faxi walked across the ice and jumped over the quickly flowing current. As the horse leaped into the air, the man's hat fell forward onto his face. The moon came out from behind a cloud and Gudrún saw his white skull.

The man said:

The moon is gliding;
Death is riding;

See the white place
On the back of my head,
Gah-roon, Gah-roon?

Gudrún was in shock and could not speak. So in silence they rode to Myrká. They dismounted when they reached the covered gate beside the church cemetery and the man said:

Wait for me here, Gah-roon, Gah-roon,
While I take my Faxi, Faxi
Beyond the hedge to the field.

And he led the horse away.

Gudrún stood frozen in horror until she spied an open grave just beyond the gate. Realizing that the man was a ghost, she turned and ran toward the church.

The ghost seized Gudrún from behind, grasping the edge of her cloak so fiercely that it tore from her at the seam of the sleeve. When Gudrún reached the safety of the church, she turned and saw the ghost leap headlong into the open grave, her cloak clutched to his side. Heaps of earth from both sides of the grave fell in over him and re-filled the hole.

Too terrified to go anywhere alone, Gudrún grabbed the church bell rope and pulled on it until she had roused all the farm folk in Myrká. She told them her story and they confirmed that indeed, the deacon was dead. She must have been travelling with his ghost.

Later that night the deacon again rose from his grave and began searching for Gudrún. He found her in her bed. Since none of the villagers were able to sleep that night, they all heard the sound of him trying to drag her away.

The deacon returned for Gudrún every night for

several weeks. But the villagers never left her alone. Not for a moment. Even the priest from a neighboring village sat with her and read from the Psalms of David to protect her from the deacon's ghostly persecution.

Finally they sent for a sorcerer from the west who was skilled in the art of witchcraft. He dug up a large stone and placed it in the middle of Gudrún's room. When the deacon's ghost arrived for his nightly haunting, the sorcerer seized him and forced him under the rock. Then the sorcerer cast a powerful spell that banished the passionate demon.

The deacon, to this day, lies in peace beneath that stone. Eventually the town of Myrká returned to its peaceful ways. Gudrún struggled to recover from her fear and sorrow, but those who knew her best say she was never the same again.

Based on Jón Árnason I, 270–272

The Ghost's Son

In ancient times, the farm at Bakki, now called Prestsbakki, in Hrútafjördur stood further north than it does today. It was originally built on a hill by the sea near Hellishólar. This is the story of how that farm became haunted and why the villagers were forced to move it to its present location.

In the old days, a priest lived at the Bakki farm. His young daughter was being courted by a farmer in the parish. When the young man eventually asked for the girl's hand in marriage, the priest refused his offer. Many times the farmer asked, but each time he was rejected. By summer, the suitor was so frustrated that he became sick and died. He was buried near the priest's house, in the graveyard of the Bakki church.

Throughout the following winter, the people of the parish began to notice that the priest's daughter was acting very strangely and no one could figure out why.

The girl knew that her foster mother was a wise woman, and eventually she decided to confide in her. She told the old woman that every night the ghost of her dead suitor visited her room. He always treated her in a tender and loving way. And although she tried, she soon grew weary of rejecting his advances and succumbed to his lovemaking. She also admitted she was pregnant with his baby. Unfortunately, the ghost had placed a curse on the child and it was destined to live an unhappy life.

After finishing her story, she begged for help. She asked her mother to somehow remove the curse and stop the ghost's nightly visits.

One warm evening, the old woman decided to confront the ghost. She strolled into the church graveyard, knitting in hand, and stopped at the young suitor's grave. Since the grave was wide open, she sat down on the edge and tossed her ball of wool into the hole. Then she began knitting, knowing that ghosts can not return to their graves if someone drops something into them. She patiently sat until the ghost finally reappeared. He immediately begged her to remove the ball of wool from his grave so he could enter his coffin and get some rest.

"I will do no such thing," the old woman said. "Unless you tell me where you go when you leave your grave each night."

"I visit the priest's daughter," the ghost answered. "The priest can not stop me from seeing her. And now, she is carrying my child. It's a boy."

"And what fate lies ahead for this child?" she asked.

"One day he will become the priest of Bakki," the ghost said. "But the first time he stands in front of the altar and blesses the congregation, the church and everyone in it will sink into hell. When this happens, my revenge against the priest for not allowing me to marry his daughter will be complete."

"What a frightful prophecy, if it really does happen," said the old woman. "Is there any way to prevent this tragedy?"

"There is only one way," said the ghost. "Someone must stab the priest while he stands at the altar, at the very moment he begins to pronounce the blessing. I don't think anyone will be brave enough to do that."

"Is that all?" she asked. "Is there no other way to end the curse?"

"No," replied the ghost. "No other way."

The old woman contemplated what the ghost had told her. Then she removed the ball of wool and said to him, "Go into your grave and never come out again."

The ghost dived into his coffin. As the ground closed over him, the old woman cast a magic spell, making certain that the ghost remained in his grave and never again haunted the area. She sadly returned home, and never told anyone about what she had learned that night.

A few months later, the girl gave birth to a fine healthy boy. The priest never knew who the boy's father was, but happily raised him on the Bakki farm. When the boy was still quite young, everyone in the parish realized that he surpassed his companions in strength and intelligence. Later, he was sent away to study, and he quickly excelled beyond the other students. Eventually, when his training ended, and the boy returned to Bakki to become his grandfather's curate.

When the boy took his grandfather's place at the parish church, the old woman realized that soon the curse would be fulfilled. She decided to confide in her son, knowing that he was a very courageous man and would never shirk his duty, especially if he knew how much was at stake.

She related the entire story of her encounter with the ghost in the graveyard. Then she begged him to kill the young priest at the moment he began his first blessing. She promised her son that she would take every punishment that might come from performing this deed.

At first her son was unwilling even to consider killing a priest. But eventually his mother's distress convinced him that her story was true, and finally he agreed to help her, swearing that he would never change his mind.

The day arrived for the young priest to perform his first church service. A large crowd had gathered and everyone was amazed to hear his sweet voice and eloquent speech. When the young man stood at the altar and raised his hands for the blessing, the old woman gave her son the signal. The unwilling man rushed forward and stabbed the priest in his heart. The priest immediately fell to the floor—dead.

Horrorstruck at what they had just witnessed, several men raced forward and seized the murderer. Several others went to help the priest but all they found was the top vertebra of his neck lying on the steps where a body should have been.

The congregation realized that what they had witnessed was no ordinary murder. The old woman stood in their midst and told them the entire story. After listening to her tale, they were filled with terror at what might have happened. They thanked her for her resourcefulness and her son for his courage.

Later the congregation noticed that the east end of the church had sunk a little way into the ground. They realized that it had begun sinking when the priest spoke the first few syllables of the blessing and stopped the moment he was killed.

Following this incident, the farm at Bakki became so haunted by ghosts that no one could live there. With the help of neighbors, it was moved to the place where it still stands to this day.

Based on Jón Árnason I, 247–275

Móri, the Ghost of Írafell

In the late 18th century, at Mödruvellir in Kjós, there lived a government official and respected farmer named Kort Thorvardarson. Kort's first wife, Ingibjörg, grew up in the north. A popular young woman, she was pursued by several suitors but always refused their offers of marriage. When she met Kort and accepted his proposal, the other men became angry and accused her of mistreating them. Although Kort was a better choice for a husband and superior to the other men in many ways, the rejected suitors allowed jealousy to overrule their better judgment. They ganged together and hired a wizard to send a ghost to haunt Kort and Ingibjörg.

To honor the rejected suitors' request, the wizard decided to bring back to life a small boy who had died of exposure in the open country. He called up the child's spirit, while his body was still warm and perhaps not completely dead, and sent him to cause trouble for Kort and Ingibjörg. The wizard also ordered the boy to remain with the couple's descendants for the next nine generations.

A description of this ghost comes from the many people who saw him throughout the years. They say he wore grey breeches with a russet-colored cloak over his shirt. He also wore a broad-brimmed black hat with a tear just above the left eye. The ghost's name was Móri, from *mór* (russet), the color of his cloak.

Móri obeyed the wizard's orders and traveled to

Mödruvellir. Once there, he began attacking the people living in the area. Then he started causing trouble for Kort and his wife, killing their livestock and spoiling their food. There are no stories of Móri killing a person, but unfortunately, animals were not so lucky. There were several strange incidents that everyone agreed were caused by this ghost.

One winter, Kort and Ingibjörg lovingly raised two orphan calves. The following summer, when they were let out to pasture, Móri chased the calves over a cliff. When the couple found the dead animals crushed on the rocks, they were heartbroken.

Another time, one of Kort's mares gave birth to a beautiful foal. The two horses contentedly grazed all summer long in the pastures near the farm. Late in the year, several men stared in disbelief as the foal suddenly went crazy and began galloping around and around a rock. As soon as the foal fell down dead, the men approached it and discovered that Móri had stuck the animal's guts to the rock. The poor foal had torn all its insides out before finally dying.

Since Móri was not completely dead when the wizard called him back to life, he, like many ghosts, needed food. That's the reason why Móri decided to haunt Ingibjörg's dairy. He would sit on a cross beam, dipping his hands into the milk churn. After playing in the milk for a while, he would splash it everywhere and fling it across the room. Then he would toss the curds, hurling them high into the rafters. He even threw turf and gravel into the dairy products to ruin every batch. Every time Ingibjörg entered the dairy, she too was drenched in milk.

To counter Móri's mischief, Ingibjörg decided to feed him at every meal. She ordered the servants to prepare him a plate, filled with all the foods that the family ate. The plate was set in the same spot each day so Móri could find it.

Once, someone forgot to feed Móri. The next morning when the servants went into the dairy, they found him squatting, balanced on the rims of two curd barrels. His hands were paddling around in the curds and he was splashing them all over the room. After that incident, no one ever forgot to feed him, and the well-fed Móri seldom spoiled the milk.

Years passed. Ingibjörg died. Kort remarried and moved to Flekkudalur, where he died in 1821.

After Kort's death, Móri attached himself to Kort's eldest son Magnús, who continued to live at Írafell. Móri haunted that farm for so long that he became known as Móri of Írafell.

When Magnús inherited the family ghost, he learned that food was not the only thing that Móri needed. He also needed a place to sleep. To keep the ghost happy, Magnús always kept an empty bed for him near his own. No one dared sleep in it, knowing that it was Móri's.

One autumn during the sheep round-up, Magnús offered the people working at Írafell food and lodging for the night. Late in the evening, a boy knocked on the door and asked for a place to stay. Magnús gladly welcomed the lad but told him that he would have to sleep on the floor or, if he was willing, sleep in Móri's bed. With no knowledge of the family ghost, the boy happily accepted the bed.

The boy settled in for the night, but the moment his eyes slammed shut, a frightening thing happened. He began to make strange rattling noises in his throat. The frightened child woke up and spent the rest of the night fending off attacks from Móri.

The next day, the weather was so bad that no one could leave the farm and the workers were forced to spend a second night there. That evening, several of the boys who lived at Írafell decided to help their guest get a good night's sleep. They were familiar with Móri's scare tactics and were often caught in mud-slinging fights with him. They placed knives all around the bed, with the sharp points facing upward. That night, the boy slept peacefully. And everyone at Írafell realized that Móri was afraid to go near the bed because of the knives.

Another time, Magnús went down to Seltjarnarnes where he knew there was a large school of fish swimming offshore. Since he did not have a fishing boat or crew of his own, he was forced to find a seat on someone else's vessel. For two days, he fished with the crew of Sigurdur of Hrólfsskáli.

The rowers on Sigurdur's boat noticed that something strange followed Magnús on board each day and never left his side. On the third morning, Magnús again boarded the boat with Móri following close behind. They were about to set out to sea when the rowers decided to speak to Sigurdur about Magnús' strange companion. They told Sigurdur that every time Magnús came on board, they saw something that looked like a ball of russet-colored wool or dried horse manure rolling on board behind him.

Sigurdur was a cautious and intelligent man. To appease his rowers he asked Magnús to leave the boat and told him that he would not take him out to sea again. No one knows if Sigurdur actually saw Móri, or if he just wanted to protect Magnús from being blamed for any bad luck his rowers might encounter while fishing. For whatever reason, Magnús was forced to find another boat and crew.

On another occasion, Magnús asked a man named
Ásgeir Finnbogason to bind some loose sheets of
Hallgrímur Pétursson's *Hymns of the Passion* for him.
One evening, after taking possession of the papers,
Ásgeir's wife decided to stay awake and greet her
husband when he returned home. At first she stayed
busy, but as the evening wore on, she grew tired and
finally went to bed. She was barely awake when her
husband arrived home. Ásgeir crawled into the bed
beside her and she sleepily blew out the light.

Peering into the darkness, Ásgeir's wife saw a
rough looking figure enter the house. It walked over
to the bed, sat on a chair, and rested its arm along the
headboard. The woman was lying on the outer side of
the bed and felt the full weight of the arm. It was so
heavy that she cried out, asking who the stranger was.
"Jón?" she asked, thinking that perhaps it was their
foster son. But the figure did not reply.

Refusing to be frightened, the woman grew angry
and again asked who dared come into their house in
the dead of night. When she again received no reply,
she told the figure to go to the lowest pit of Hell.

Suddenly the figure stood up. In the moonlight
from the window, its eyes glinted like a cat's eyes. A
shelf, in the opposite corner of the room tumbled to
the floor with a horribly loud crash. The shelf was
laden with books and dishes, and when it fell, the
sheets of Hallgrímur Pétursson's *Hymns* scattered
across the floor.

The frightened mistress of the house relit the
lamp. The ghost disappeared, but she spent the rest of
the night wide awake. Early the next morning,
Magnús arrived and asked for the bound sheets of the
Hymns. Members of the household recounted the

night's events to him and said that he had quite an unpleasant ghost for a companion.

Móri also liked to haunt Einar, another of Kort's sons. One early winter day, Einar decided to travel to Kjós to visit some relatives. He walked along the coast road and across Kollafjördur. As dusk fell, he approached Kjalarnes but rather than stop for the night, he pressed on, arriving at his destination long after bedtime.

Einar was no stranger to the household. But instead of waking everyone up, he decided to sleep in the cow house. He found an empty stall, settled in and peacefully slept until morning.

Waking early, Einar went to the house to tell his family that he had arrived. After a hearty greeting, he told them that he had spent the night in the cow house and he hoped that they didn't mind.

The men said that he should have come into the house. He would have been most welcome, no matter how late the hour. Then they told Einar that by coming the way he did, he caused more trouble for them than if he had woken them up. That morning, their best cow was found lying, with her neck broken, in the same stall next to where he had slept the night before. Apparently Móri had decided to make room for his master by killing the cow so Einar would have a place to sleep.

There are other stories about Írafell's Móri. For generations, this ghost haunted the family, causing disruptions in their lives and bothering everyone around them.

Based on Jón Árnason I, 364–373

Selsmóri, the Ghost of Selur

There once was a farmer and his wife who lived at Bústadir at the mouth of the Hellirá River. The farmer hired a worker named Thorgardur and allowed him to live in their house. Soon rumors began to spread that the farmer's wife was cheating on him. When the gossip reached the farmer, he confronted Thorgardur. The two men fought over the woman, and the farmer lost.

Losing the dispute forced the farmer to accept that his wife belonged to another man. But to make matters worse, while Thorgardur stayed safe and warm at home, the farmer had to do all the difficult and dangerous jobs on the farm. One of those jobs was tending the sheep herds during the winter months when the weather was violent and unpredictable.

One winter morning, the farmer set off to tend the sheep, telling the household that he would return in the evening. Later that day, a blizzard caught him by surprise and he was stranded in the storm.

Back at the farm, the household waited anxiously for his return. The night passed slowly, but without a sign of him. When the farmer did not return home by the following evening, a search party was organized. They set out at dawn and a little while later found his dead body in the river. The farmer's body was covered in wounds and everyone agreed that his death must have been at human hands.

The rumors about Thorgardur and the farmer's wife quickly fueled the belief that he was the murderer. The case was examined and every piece of evidence seemed to point to him. Thorgardur vehemently denied causing his master's death, but still he was condemned to die by hanging. The only way he could save his life was by paying a very high fee. Since Thorgardur did not have the money, he searched for a man willing to pay his fine.

At that time, a rich man named Jón lived at Selur in Seltjarnarnes. Thorgardur went to Jón and begged him to pay the fine and free him from certain death. At first, Jón was reluctant to help but Thorgardur continued to plead, promising to serve him and his family loyally for as long as youth and strength permitted.

Jón listened to the man's appeal and was persuaded to help. He sat down at the table and began counting coins. When he was nearly finished, his wife Gudrún entered the room and asked him what he was doing with all the money. Jón told her that he was going to use it to pay Thorgardur's fine.

Gudrún was incensed. How could he make such a stupid mistake? She knew the man's story; he was not worth sparing from the noose. She rushed to her husband's side and lifting the corners of her pinafore, swept her hand across the table and pushed the coins into it.

Jón watched in stunned silence as his wife angrily said that she was going to keep the money. Then she turned to Thorgardur and said, "Every man must suffer the consequences of his own actions."

"Very well," said Thorgardur. "But you too will face the consequences of your actions. I will haunt you and your descendants for the next nine generations." And he turned and left their house.

Some time later, Thorgardur was executed for the crime he claimed that he did not commit. No one is sure where the execution took place. Some say it was in Kópavógur, others say it was elsewhere in Iceland, or even abroad. No matter where he died, Thorgardur's ghost returned to Selur and haunted Gudrún and Jón for the rest of their lives. As promised, the ghost's vengeance was especially vicious toward Gudrún. He enjoyed causing Gudrún to hallucinate and driving her completely crazy.

Because Thorgardur spent most of his time at Selur, he became known as Selsmóri, or Móri of Selur. But sometimes he preferred that people call him Thorgardur, his name when he was alive.

Gudrún and Jón had one daughter whom they named Thorgerdur (which one might have thought would be enough to appease the ghost). She married an important farmer from Skildinganes named Halldór Bjarnason. When Gudrún and Jón died, Halldór inherited the farm at Selur, and that inheritance included Selsmóri.

Little is mentioned about Selsmóri during the lifetimes of Thorgerdur and Halldór. He was also quiet during the lifetime of their son, Bjarni, a man of great achievement. Although Selsmóri did not make his presence known at Skildinganes very often, everyone knew he was around and he stayed as long as Bjarni's descendents lived there.

Bjarni's children were all very accomplished people. His second daughter, Thurídur, married a priest named Benedikt Björnsson. Although Thurídur was an intelligent woman, she suffered from bouts of insanity. Selsmóri, the family ghost, was blamed for her illness and the divorce that occurred because of it.

During one of her insanity attacks, Thurídur was reported to have said, "My sister, there is a snake biting me!" Others say she said, "Ingibjörg is always stabbing me in the heart with a shoe nail." Some people think she was referring to a woman who lived with her and Benedikt before their divorce. (And since Ingibjörg later became Benedikt's second wife, maybe there was a more earthly reason for Thurídur's madness.)

Luckily the illness was not a family weakness, even though some people claimed that certain members of the family were a bit temperamental and eccentric.

There is no mention of Selsmóri haunting Thurídur's sister, Ragnheidur. But some hold Selsmóri responsible for the death of Ragnheidur's first husband. He drowned in 1817, when his post ship sank off the coast of Snæfellsnes in the south of Iceland. And perhaps, Selsmóri had something to do with the death of her brother, Thórdur, as well.

Selsmóri played tricks on each generation of this family. And the stories continue. Who knows—maybe he is still haunting them today.

Based on Jón Árnason I, 373–376

The Hauntings at Stokkseyri

This story begins on March 29, 1892, at the end of a winter's day of fishing. The sky was dark and threatening when ten strong and healthy fishermen settled in for the night. They were all together in a small shelter with a door that opened toward the sea.

As the wind and rain moved in, their foreman, a man named Sigurdur Henriksson, entertained them with stories. At about ten o'clock, the foreman left and his men bolted the door behind him.

The shelter was made up of one room, except for a small recess near the door where they kept their fishing gear. There were two bunks along the wall by the doors and three bunks opposite them on the north side. The men slept two to a bunk, in opposite directions, head to foot.

All the men fell asleep except two. Eyjólfur Ólafsson was one of the men who stayed awake. He is also the one who recounted the story.

Eyjólfur was talking to his companion when all of a sudden one of the other men started making weird noises. They immediately thought that the ghost Skerflóds-Móri was bothering their friend.

Skerflóds-Móri was a well-known ghost who was attached to the members of a family from that district. And everyone knew it liked to attack men, in a very fiendish way—in their dreams.

Eyjólfur woke the man and asked him to recount

his dream. The man said that he hadn't been dreaming, but had experienced a strange and unpleasant sensation. While that man was still speaking, one of the other sleeping men began to behave in the same manner, whimpering pathetically, and frightening everyone who was awake. Quickly, they lit a lamp and searched the entire hut, trying to find the ghost.

When no ghost was found, Eyjólfur returned to his bunk, one of the three that were on the north side of the hut. He waited, and soon in one of the bunks near the door sat up and grabbed for a box of snuff. The moment he took a pinch, his skin paled, and his hands fell loosely into his lap. Without warning, his face started to turn blue and his head began to swell. At first he cried out, but then just whimpered pathetically.

Only Eyjólfur leaped out of bed and ran to the man's side, to try to help.

A short while later, the man recovered. He told Eyjólfur that as he pinched the snuff, a terrible heaviness overwhelmed him. All strength drained out of his body and he could not move or even cry for help, except for the pathetic whimper that they'd heard. After that, he had lost consciousness.

The men were frightened by what they had witnessed. So they climbed out of bed, got dressed and sat down to play a game of cards, believing that if they stayed awake, the ghost would stay away. Several of the men tried to get some sleep, but the moment they closed their eyes, they were overcome with the same horrible heaviness that had attacked their friends.

The men decided not to tell anyone about their nighttime experiences. They wanted to wait and see if it happened again. Unfortunately, the very next night, it did. The ghost reappeared and attacked any man who fell asleep. The fishermen even tried reading aloud from Hallgrímur Pétursson's *Hymns of the Passion*, but it didn't stop the ghost. Every time they started to read, a black fly would settle on the book and walked over the words so no one could see them.

The next day, the men decided to borrow the bell from Stokkseyri church. They wanted to know if their ghost was strong enough to attack them in the presence of a holy church bell. That night, with the bell hanging near by, the ghost stayed away. Relieved, the men thought their troubles were over and they returned the bell to the church.

Sadly, they rejoiced too soon. For the very next night, the ghost returned and devilishly disturbed every man in the hut. For five nights in a row, the ghost viciously haunted them.

Finally, when they could stand it no longer, they took refuge at the farm where their foreman lived. Although they slept in comfort, the haunting ghost was busy disrupting the sleep of other fisherman on farms throughout the district. The hauntings became so intense that one by one the other fisherman's huts were abandoned. For five or six weeks, the ghost travelled from hut to hut attacking any sleeping occupant.

Skerflóds-Móri was often seen through the windows of the huts, looking like "a lump with some kind of tentacles attached. Tentacles that fastened onto the window pane as if struggling to get inside." There are several other descriptions of Skerflóds-Móri, but this isn't surprising since ghosts can assume a variety of shapes and sizes. Eyjólfur said that several of his hut-mates described their ghost as "a blue vapor, moving back and forth. Sometimes glowing and accompanied by a strange wind and sudden chill in the air." Others reported that the ghost was, "a thick blue cloud, about an ell high."

Still others said it appeared as "a lump, about the size of a small dog."

Some people speculated that these strange hauntings were not the work of Skerflóds-Móri. A few men thought they were caused by a monster that rose out of the sea. Others thought it was a ghost from the Mosfell district that was sent to attack someone but had lost its way. Still others argued that it must be Stokkseyri-Dísa, a ghost that was thought to have been laid to rest long ago on a hill near the fishermen's shelter. Stokkseyri-Dísa had been ordered to stay in her grave as long as the hill was not disturbed. But someone had decided recently removed several stones from the hill used them to build a stable wall. That decision must have released the ghost to wander throughout the district.

Although several people in the area were eager to learn the truth about this evil ghost, everyone agreed that it was far more important to find a way to get rid of it. They had to stop the hauntings or all the fisherman's huts would be abandoned and the ghost would turn its attention to the farms.

But how do you get rid of such a troublesome ghost?

The Stokkseyri church bell was one way to protect a hut. But it could only be in one place at a time. Avoiding the bell, the ghost could jump from hut to hut, causing as much trouble as before.

In desperation, the fishermen called for a doctor and the local sheriff. They hoped that if the ghost was confronted by someone in authority, it could go away. The two men examined the huts, but they never found the ghost and their visit did not reduce the number of hauntings.

The men also lost their faith in the effectiveness of godly words for when they read from *The Hymns of the Passion,* it didn't stop the ghost. This probably explains why they didn't call in a priest to perform an exorcism or pray over each hut.

Time passed, and the men despaired of ever getting rid of the evil fiend. In the spring, a man named Eyjólfur Magnússon visited Eyrarbakki. He was known throughout the area as a man of power and insight. The fishermen approached him and begged for his help to get rid of their ghost. They told him they were willing to pay any price for his services.

At first, Eyjólfur refused to listen to their request. But the men were persistent and eventually he agreed to get rid of the ghost, at least for a while.

Eyjólfur uttered powerful words over the ghost and sent it north to the island of Drangey for the next nine years. One of the verses he chanted was:

I conjure thee, to men's content,
Devil in a jerkin (jacket),
North the next nine years now sent,
Drangey's Isle to lurk in.

Eyjólfur could guarantee them a respite of only nine years and the people of Stokkseyri should plan for another ghostly visit some time in the future.

Based on Jón Yorkelsson, 385–389

The Hairy Man at Skardi

This story happened a long time ago on one of the beaches of Medalland. Medalland was an area in Iceland where the bodies of people who drowned at sea were often washed ashore. Usually, the bodies were the drowned crew members from a shipwreck off the coast. Sometimes discovering where the dead men came from was an impossible task.

One day the body of an unusual man—some tales say two men—washed ashore. To everyone's surprise, he was not wearing any clothes and his body was completely covered with hair. He had long claws on every finger and every toe.

The people who found this strange creature were frightened by it. But like so many times before, they carried the body to a nearby farm, built a coffin, and placed him inside. The coffin was then carried to the church for burial.

At the time, there was a church and graveyard at Skardi. Unfortunately, sandstorms destroyed them both, along with all the property. So today this site is no longer visible.

The funeral service started and the congregation picked up their hymnals and turned to the first hymn. As they looked down at the words, something strange began to happen. Every letter on the page turned back to front and twisted into forms of blasphemy and curses. The pcople were so confused that no one was able to sing. The service was further disrupted when the priest began to perform a blessing over the body. As the words of the blessing passed his lips, they turned into profanity. He was so perplexed that he had to stop. Still, in spite of these strange happenings, the body was buried in holy ground.

Everyone tried to guess who the strange man was. Some thought he was a pirate, guilty of kidnapping Icelanders. Others thought he might be a spirit in human form or some species of ape.

Not long after the funeral, the people began to notice unusual ghostly activity around the Skardi church. As the activity increased, the people became frightened and found it impossible to travel through the area after dark. What they saw was Hairy Man (their name for the newly buried body) banging on the church with planks from his coffin.

An interesting thing happened after the burial of the Hairy Man. It became very easy for a person to get lost in the area known as Kirkjumelar or Church Sands. Most people now travel on the well-marked trail that runs between the Hnausar and Langholt farms, but part of the Kirkjumelar trail passes by the spot where the Skardi church once stood. There are many stories of people approaching this area and losing their way, especially when the clouds hang low or severe weather darkens the sky. Sometimes even horses get nervous and uncertain about which way to go.

Here are a couple of Hairy Man stories:

Long ago, there lived a priest at Hnausar named Jón. One winter day, he was travelling home and decided to go through Medalland. It was late in the evening and the low-hanging clouds made for poor visibility. But the priest knew the area like the back of his hand and he was not concerned when darkness fell. Unfortunately, when he started along the Kirkjumelar trail, he quickly lost his way and wandered around the sands for most of the night.

Back at the rectory, they were anticipating his return. When he was overdue, they placed a light in a window, knowing that he could see it from a long distance and easily follow it home.

At dawn, a dazed and exhausted priest finally reached the rectory. When he was asked why he didn't follow the light, he sighed and said, "There were so many lights! Only the Devil himself would have known which one was the right one to follow!"

Another Hnausar man, named Stefan, had lived his entire life on the farm. He knew how easy it was for people to lose their way while travelling along the Kirkjumelar trail. It made him very unhappy when travellers passed by on their way south and insisted on continuing their journey when the weather was uncertain or it was late at night. Finally, he refused to allow anyone, especially those who lived and worked on the farm, to travel from the Hnausar farm under those conditions.

Late one afternoon, a traveller arrived at Hnausar farm. He told Stefan that he was planning to continue south to Langholt, and if possible even further. The weather was good, but a light snow was falling. Stefan firmly advised his guest not to go any further, but the man refused to listen. Stefan begged him not to go, but the traveller had made up his mind.

As they parted, Stefan said, "I see that I can not change your mind, but please remember, stay north of the poles. Be careful that you do not go south of them."

The man thanked him for his advice, said goodbye

and continued his journey. The man's journey passed without any mishaps, but he heeded Stefan's advice and did not stray into the land of the Hairy Man.

One winter night, a man was travelling across Medalland with his three horses. It was late in the evening and so dark that he could not see very far in front of him. The man was not worried about the poor visibility because he was riding the oldest of his horses, a mare that was sure-footed, well-travelled, and not easily frightened. He considered her the very best of animals. The younger horses, however, were more headstrong, so he kept them close by his side.

Their journey passed without incident until they started along the Kirkjumelar trail, and his horse wandered off the path. Suddenly, she stopped in her tracks and began to violently tremble. The man tried to calm her, but soon all three horses were very frightened. The younger ones reared up onto their hind legs, leaping about, and kicking in all directions. The older horse remained paralyzed, not moving a single inch.

The man did all that he could to calm the horses. He encouraged them to move on, but their weird behavior continued. Finally, he became so furious that he jumped off the horse and started running in circles around them, hitting the sand and the air with his whip. Completely exhausted, he grabbed the bridle of the oldest horse and started walking, leading the horses for quite a distance before they finally calmed down.

Some time later, he found the trail that ran north of the poles. Only then did the horses relax, and he was able to mount and continue on his journey.

Based on Einar Guðmundsson I, 16–18

Mela-Manga

If anything strange or frightening happened in Medalland, the Hairy Man at Skardi was usually blamed for it. But he wasn't the only ghost who haunted that region—some of the incidents could be attributed to the work of Mela-Manga.

One winter day, a long time ago, a young girl named Margrét was travelling between farms. She carried a set of knitting needles and like so many women of her day passed the time knitting woolen socks and scarves. Because the weather was warm, a blanket of fog settled over the region, enveloping Margrét. She quickly became confused and lost her way. No one knows exactly what happened to her, but many believe that she died of exposure.

Her accident, like so many before it, was blamed on the Hairy Man.

But young Margrét refused to rest in peace. Her spirit haunted the region, creating mischief wherever and whenever possible. Visitors and residents often saw her on the Medalland sands, carrying a half-finished sock and frantically knitting a new one. She was soon nicknamed Mela-Manga, a combination of the words *melar* (sand plains) and Manga, a shortened version of Margrét.

Many people have said that even when they couldn't see Mela-Manga, they could hear the click, click, click of her knitting needles or sense her eerie presence.

Mela-Manga's favorite pastime was playing with shepherds. She loved to trick them into thinking that rocks or patches of flowers were actually their sheep. When the shepherds finally caught up with what they thought were stray animals, they were annoyed to discover that they had been chasing illusions.

One time a man named Sigurdur was living at Botnar in Medalland. He was watching over his sheep as a storm slowly moved into the area. Snow began to fall and soon it was so heavy that Sigurdur grew confused and lost his way.

Suddenly, from every direction he heard a voice whisper, "Siggi, Siggi, Siggi, Siggi!"

Now Sigurdur was usually a calm man. But as the voice continued its repetitious murmuring, he lost his patience and called out in a nasty voice, "Well, you devil! At least I know that you know my name!"

Immediately, the whispering stopped and the fog lifted. Sigurdur found his way back home, certain in the knowledge that Mela-Manga had tried to trick him.

Based on Einar Guðmundsson I, 19

Skotta, the Ghost from Móhús

On a now deserted farm at Refstokkur, there once lived a rich farmer named Jón Thordarsson. Although he was born into a poor family, he cleverly hoarded enormous amounts of money. With his money, Jón bought land. Any time a piece of property in the area went up for sale, he purchased it, usually managing to negotiate a very low price.

One day a young girl came to Jón's farm, begging for a safe and warm place to spend the night. Jón angrily ordered her to leave his land and continue her journey. Later that evening, the girl died of exposure.

In time, the girl's spirit rose from the grave and began to haunt Jón. She followed him everywhere, playing tricks on him whenever possible. She even followed him when he moved to the tiny Móhús farm in the Stokkseyri region.

The ghost's name was Skotta, and she loved to disrupt Jón's life by killing both his and his neighbor's livestock. Her vicious attacks followed Jón whenever he travelled. She even chewed apart his socks and shoes while they were still on his feet. Time after time, she chomped at the heels of his socks or munched through the laces on his shoes. Any morning that Jón pulled on a new pair of socks, he knew they would be in pieces by the evening.

Skotta also liked to strangle Jón. She tried so often that he resorted to tying a long cord through the button holes in his shirt collar to make it harder for her to tighten it around his neck.

Things got even worse when Skotta teamed up with Selsmóri, the ghost of Selur.

One winter, just before Christmas, a man named Tómas travelled to Stokkseyri to buy a leg of smoked lamb for his festival meal. He purchased his meat and toward evening set off for home. In the morning, travellers found his bruised and bloody body, torn to pieces, a short distance from where Skotta had died of exposure.

After Tómas' death, the people of the region began to see three ghosts where originally there had been only Selsmóri and Skotta. Everyone was sure that the new ghost was Tómas. The three ghosts joined forces and the area became so haunted that nobody dared travel from dusk until dawn. Everyone feared that they might get lost in the dark and end up in the hands of this trio of ghosts.

Since his ghost, Skotta, was the meanest of the three, Jón finally decided that he was the one who should find someone who could send all the ghosts back to their graves. He travelled east, found a magician, and reluctantly offered to pay him thirty dollars if he could end the haunting and free Jón from the troublesome Skotta. After paying the magician half of the money in advance, Jón returned home.

The magician quickly travelled west. He located the ghost of Tómas and sent him quietly back into his grave. After an exhaustive search for Selsmóri, the magician realized that the ghost had vanished. And, since no one heard from him again, the magician decided that he too was safely vanquished.But when he found Skotta, he decided to take her back home with him to eastern Iceland.

The magician went to Jón and asked for the second half of his money. Jón refused to pay him, arguing that since he had not vanquished Selsmóri, he did not fulfill his part of their agreement. The magician disagreed. He had removed two of the ghosts and even though he couldn't find Selsmóri, the ghost was no longer haunting the area. He had stopped the hauntings and expected to be paid. After a heated argument, the greedy Jón still refused to pay another cent and the unhappy magician returned home.

Stories filtered back to the region that Skotta almost drowned the magician, along with the crew of the Sandhólar ferry, as they travelled across the Thjórsá River. Still other stories said that once the magician and the ghost reached eastern Iceland, the magician got so irratated with Skotta's behavior, he forced her back into her grave.

Based on Jón Árnason I, 347–348

FOUR

Water Monsters

The Merman Laughs

Long ago in Vogar there lived a farmer who was also a strong and experienced fisherman. One day while out fishing, he cast his line over the side of the boat and patiently waited for a fish to grab it. When nothing happened, he gave the line a tug and discovered that something heavy was weighing it down. After a bit of a struggle, he managed to move whatever was hanging on the line. When his catch reached the surface, the farmer was amazed to see a gigantic fish-like being, attached to his hook! It had the head and body of a man and the tail of a fish.

Once the farmer realized that the creature was still alive, he said, "Who are you? Where did you come from?"

"I am a merman," the fish replied. "I live at the bottom of the sea."

The farmer asked him what he had been doing when the hook grabbed into his flesh.

"I was turning the cover on my mother's chimney to increase the draft," he said. "Will you please let me go?"

"Not yet," said the farmer. "First you must serve me."

After dragging the merman out of the water and into his boat, the farmer rowed back to shore. When they reached the boathouse, the farmer's dog rushed out and joyfully greeted his master. The dog barked and danced all around, wagging his tail and begging for attention. The farmer lost his temper with the dog and kicked the poor animal out of his way.

The merman laughed.

After securing his boat, the farmer grabbed his prize catch and started to drag it toward home. As they crossed a field, the man stumbled over a rock and cursed it, demanding to know why fate had placed it on his land.

The merman laughed for the second time.

When the farmer arrived home, his wife greeted him with kisses and hugs. She was a very affectionate woman and the farmer lovingly returned her embrace.

The merman laughed for the third time.

Turning his attention to the merman, the farmer said, "You have laughed at me three times. I am curious to know why—so tell me."

"No," replied the merman. "Not unless you promise to set me free, and return me to the exact spot where I was caught."

The farmer agreed.

"Well," said the merman. "What I laughed at was your stupidity. The first time because you struck a dog whose only fault was greeting you with joy and sincere affection. The second time when you cursed a rock that was covering a treasure just waiting to be discovered. The third time when you accepted the loving greeting of a wife who is a fraud and unfaithful to you. Now, be an honest man and return me to the sea."

"Two of the things you mentioned I have no way of proving—the faithfulness of my dog and the unfaithfulness of my wife," the farmer replied. "But I can verify the truth of the third, the treasure that you say is buried on my land. If the treasure exists, I will believe what you say about my dog and my wife."

The farmer went to the hill and dug under the rock. Deep in the ground he found a vast treasure of gold, exactly where the merman said it would be buried. As promised, he carried the merman back to the sea and released him in exactly the same spot where he had found him.

Before the merman jumped into the water, he said to the farmer, "You are an honest man and I will reward you for returning me safely to my mother. I will send you a gift, but you must be skilled enough to take possession of it when it arrives. Be happy and prosper!"

Not long after, seven sea-gray cows, with bladders hanging from their noses, appeared on the beach near the farmer's land. The cows were very wild, and when the farmer tried to approach them, they charged! The farmer grabbed a stick and faced them—head on. He was convinced that the cows were the promised gift from the merman. He figured that if he broke the bladders that hung from each cow's nose, that cow would have to live on land and thus belong to him.

The farmer swatted at the bladder of the first cow and broke it. The bladder split open, and the cow grew quiet enough for him to catch. Once the first cow was tamed, the others leaped back into the sea. To the farmer's delight, the tame cow turned out to be a very useful gift. She was the best looking and best milking cow in all the land. Eventually, she became the mother of a race of gray cows that are still admired today.

The farmer prospered, though he never caught another merman. As for his wife—she was never mentioned again.

Based on Jón Árnason I, 127–128

The Mermaid of Slettusand

At one time, there lived a wealthy farmer at Eyri on Reydarfjördur. He had two children: a son named Jón and a daughter named Gudrún. Jón was a quiet and prudent man and Gudrún was a beautiful woman, thought to be the best match in the community.

On the north side of the fjord, at Bakkagerdi, there lived a well-respected farmer, whose son Árni was an impetuous fellow, noisy and rude.

When Árni was still a young man, he formed a friendship with Jón and Gudrún. The three were about the same age and as they grew into adulthood, Árni often travelled to Eyri to visit them. It was a long and difficult journey that circled over the head of the fjord and crossed a strip of sand called Slettusand, after the Sletta farm that stood a short distance away.

In time, Árni fell in love with Gudrún and asked for her hand in marriage. Since he was a good-looking and wealthy young man, Gudrún, with her father's blessing, accepted his proposal.

When Árni's father heard about his son's decision to marry, he said to him, sadly, "The girl is beautiful and a good match for you. But somehow, my heart is full of doubt over this union."

Árni ignored his father's misgivings and continued to visit his betrothed and her brother.

At about this time, the people near Slettusand began to notice a little girl moving about on the sands.

She came in the evenings, just as darkness fell and the moon was shining bright. About ten years old, the girl's favorite pastime was throwing a pebble into the air and hitting it with another pebble as it fell to the ground. No one bothered the child, but she was regularly seen by people living in the neighborhood and travellers crossing the sands.

When Árni's father heard about this girl, he wondered if she was a mermaid, trying to entice a person to approach her. He warned his impetuous son, "Stay away from her! As long as you do not approach the mermaid of your own free will, she can not harm you." He warned the young man over and over about the dangers of the mermaid. Árni promised his father that he would not go near the creature.

A short time later, the two fathers met at the church in Holmar. Árni's father asked Jón's father to allow his son to travel across the sands with Árni on the evenings when he was returning home late. He wanted Jón to make sure that his often reckless son did not approach the mermaid. Jón's father agreed and from then on, Jón walked home with Árni.

The two young men spotted the little girl each time they crossed the sands. They always passed without going near her and she never seemed to notice them. It wasn't long before Árni began to talk about the girl, wondering if she truly was dangerous. He suggested that they pass a bit closer to her and find out for themselves. While Jón refused to consider this suggestion, Árni soon convinced himself that the girl was harmless.

One evening during the Lenten season, when the weather was fine and the moon was bright, the two young men crossed the sands as usual. They saw the girl throwing stones in the air and Árni repeated his suggestion about walking closer to her. He suggested that it might be amusing to meet this strange girl.

"Listen to your father's warning," said Jón. "If you don't, there could be trouble."

"There is no danger," Árni said, laughing at his friend. "Let's go near her and see what happens."

"I'm not going with you," said Jón. "If you refuse to take the advice of your father, that's your decision."

Árni turned away from Jón and ran across the sands to where the child was throwing stones. He grabbed her and said, "What are you doing here, child?"

Jón stood watching, in helpless horror, as the little girl ballooned to an enormous size, seized Árni in her arms and ran toward the sea. Before he could even cry out, she plunged into the water and disappeared from sight.

Jón ran home and told his father what had happened. Everyone was grief-stricken over Árni's fate. Not long after she heard the news, Gudrún died of a broken heart.

When word of Árni's death reached his father, he said, "I feared this might happen, but no man can avoid his fate." The death of his son broke the old man's heart, too, and he spent most of the winter in bed.

When he finally recovered, he repeatedly asked if anyone had seen the mermaid. "I will not live long," he said. "It doesn't matter if I die the same way as my son."

Three years after Árni's disappearance, the little girl again reappeared on the sands, throwing stones for her amusement. News of her return reached Árni's father at his home in Bakkagerdi. He immediately went to his smithy and forged a weapon.

One evening, not long afterward, he left home alone. No one knows what happened later that night down on the shore but by the following morning, he was back in his bed. All he said was that his son's death was avenged and no one should worry about the mermaid ever again.

"She touched me," he said. "And that touch will kill me." The old man lay in his bed for another week before he died.

Everyone in the parish grieved the loss of this loving father. He was long remembered as a wise and honest person who always accepted his fellow man.

Based on Boucher II, 75–78

Nennir, the Water Horse

Water horses (*nykur* or *nennir*) live in the waters of Iceland—in rivers, lakes, and the open sea. Though they are able to change into any shape, they usually look like an ordinary horse with a gray coat. The only unusual thing about them is that their hoofs are turned backwards on their legs and the tufts on their pasterns, just above their hoofs, also point the wrong way.

In the winter, when cracks appear in the ice and cause loud booming noises, everyone says it is a water horse neighing. The horses usually breed with other water horses, but occasionally one of their foals is born to a land mare. These foals are easily recognized because whenever someone tries to ride them or lead them through deep water they try to lie down.

Water horses often appear near rivers or lakes that are difficult to cross. By pretending to be docile, they tempt people to try to pass through the water on their backs. As soon as they have a rider, they rush into the water, dive down, and drown their passengers.

The water horse also hates to hear its name. Whenever they hear "Nykur" or "Nennir," they violently shy away and gallop into the nearest water.

All over Iceland, people believe in water horses. In almost every district, there are stories of such horses living nearby, especially near water with a very strong current.

One story, from the island of Grímsey off the northern coast, tells how their water horse always seemed to know when cows were being shipped over from the mainland. The horse's neighing would drive the cows mad and they would fling themselves into the sea and drown. As a result, the men of Grímsey never raised cows on the island until sometime in the mid-19th century.

One time, a shepherd girl was searching for her lost sheep. After travelling a long distance, she grew very tired. Suddenly, to her delight, a gray horse appeared at her side. She formed a makeshift bridle and put it in the horse's mouth. Then she placed her apron across the animal's back and led him to a clump of grass. As she was about to mount the horse, she said, "For some reason I feel afraid to mount this horse. I'm such a ninny!"

At the sound of the word "ninny," the horse violently pulled away from her. It ran to a nearby lake and disappeared into the water.

The girl watched the horse vanish and realized that she had almost ridden a water horse.

Another time, a gray horse stood quietly by as several children played on the smooth gravel shore of a lake near their farm. The children ventured over to take a closer look at the animal and one of them bravely climbed onto its back. One by one, the children climbed on for a ride, leaving only the oldest child standing on the ground. They urged him to jump on, saying that there was plenty of room on the old packhorse. The boy refused and the other children began calling him a ninny.

The horse heard the word "ninny" and hurled itself into the lake, carrying all the children with him.

The oldest child ran home and told everyone his frightening story. The horse and the children were never seen again. People in the area knew that it was Nennir, the water horse, who drowned their children.

Now it happened that a farmer in the parish of Bardur in the Fljót district decided to build a wall around the churchyard. Early one morning, the men gathered for work. The only one missing was an old man who was mean and disliked by everyone.

Around midday, the men began to mutter and moan. The old man was taking too long to get there and they were angry because by arriving late, he wasn't doing his share of the work.

On the stroke of noon, he finally arrived, leading a gray horse. He approached the group of men and was greeted with angry words from those who had worked since early morning. The old man kept his temper and simply asked what they wanted him to do. He was sent to join the group that was carrying building materials for the wall.

The old man's horse was vicious toward the other men and horses. He often broke out of line, biting and kicking anyone who came near him. The workers thought that the animal was a nuisance and decided to weigh him down with a heavy load. But it was no use. Even with loads twice as heavy as what the other horses carried, the old man's horse kept going, threatening anyone who came near and driving the other horses away.

Soon, only the old man and his horse were left to finish the work. While the other men watched, he piled materials onto his horse's back. When he was finished, the load was bigger and heavier than the combined loads of all the other horses. The animal remained quiet, allowing the man to load him and guide him wherever he wished. Using only the one gray horse, all the building materials were carried down to the churchyard.

When the job was finished, the old man took the bridle off the horse. Standing by the newly finished wall, he slapped the animal on the haunches, signaling that it was free to go. But the horse didn't like being swatted. It lifted up its hind legs and smashed both heels into the wall. The horse knocked a great big hole into the section the men had just spent the entire day building.

From that moment on, no matter how often they rebuilt that section of the wall, it would not stand. In the end, the men of the parish decided to use the hole as a gateway to the church.

Everyone realized that the old man's horse was a water horse. And indeed, the last time they saw it was when it galloped off and plunged into Hólmsvatn Lake.

Based on several legends from Jón Árnason I, 129–132

Better a Seal Skin than a Child

Legend says that the seals originated in ancient Egypt at the time when Pharaoh pursued Moses and the Jews across the Red Sea. Pharaoh and all his men drowned and became seals, which is why seal bones are so like human bones. Since that time, the seals live as a special race on the ocean floor. They have completely human shapes and personalities under their seal skins. One gift granted to them is that on Midsummer Night, some say Twelfth Night, they can put aside their seal skins, take on human form, and sing and dance the night away.

One Midsummer Night, a man was walking along the seashore and stumbled upon a group of naked people lying on the sand. He noticed that each person had a seal skin next to them. Thinking that this was very strange, he decided to venture closer and find out what was happening. He walked among the group and quickly grabbed one of the pelts. The instant he touched it, the sleeping people jumped up, slipped into their seal skins, and dived into the sea.

Within moments, the beach was empty except for one woman. She was frightened because she could not find her skin. When she saw that the man was holding it in his hand, she begged him to give it back. He refused to give it to her, but offered instead to take her to his home. The naked woman had no choice but to accept his offer.

The seal woman lived in the man's house and slowly adapted to her new life. The two eventually fell in love and married. Life was good for the couple, blessing them with seven beautiful children. The woman slowly took over the management of their house and did such a wonderful job that her husband entrusted her with all the household keys.

There was, however, one key that he did not give her. That key opened an old chest tucked away in the smithy shop. Curiously drawn to the chest, the woman often asked her husband to open it. He refused and told her that it was filled with nothing but rubbish and old tools.

Several years passed. One day, the farmer had to leave home and travel some distance away. The moment he was out of sight, his wife began looking for the key to the mysterious chest. Discouraged, she walked into the smithy shop, pulled out the chest and asked her eldest son if he had ever opened it. The boy told her that he had not.

"Do you know where the key is?" she asked.

"Father always carries it with him when he is at home," the boy replied. "When he goes away, he hides it in a hole in the wall."

"Will you please find the key for me?" begged the boy's mother.

The boy did as his mother asked and found the key. He gave it to her and she quickly opened the chest. Inside she found her seal skin. She said to her son, "Better a seal skin than a child. The skin is silent, but the child speaks."

She grabbed the skin and ran toward the sea. When she reached the water's edge, she felt a pull from deep in the ocean. She cried out, "I am so unhappy. I have seven children calling for me from the sea and seven children on the land. What a difficult choice I must make!"

The oldest boy followed his mother to the beach and realized that she was planning to put on her skin and leave their family. He begged her not to go, but in the end, she chose to put on her skin and return to her home in the sea.

Based on Jón Árnason III, 10–11

The Lagarfljót Serpent

A long time ago, a woman lived on a farm in the district near Lagarfljót Lake. One day, she gave her grown-up daughter a golden ring.

The girl said to her mother, "What shall I do with this gold?"

"Lay it under a snake," was the mother's reply.

The girl caught a snake, put the gold ring in her trinket box, and placed the snake on top of it. The serpent stayed in the box for several days. When the girl returned, it had grown so large that the side panels of the box were beginning to burst apart. Frightened of the huge creature, she grabbed the box and hurled it, with all its contents, into Lagarfljót.

A long time passed and people in the area began to notice that a large serpent was living in their lake. It was killing men and animals whenever they tried to cross over the water. Sometimes, it would crawl onto the shore and spew a horrid poison. The serpent was causing a great deal of trouble and no one knew how to get rid of it.

Finally, the residents begged two men from the north of Scandinavia, magicians known as Finns, (though probably from the Sami people of Lapland), to come and help rid the lake of the horrible beast. If they were successful in killing the serpent, they could keep all the gold that was piled up under it.

The men dived into the water but quickly

reappeared on the surface. They announced to the anxious people that they were no match for such a giant creature. They also said that there was a second, far bigger, snake laying over the pile of gold. The divers could neither kill the serpenst nor retrieve the gold. Instead, they bound the snakes with two ropes; one behind each head and one near each tail.

The serpents could no longer harm anyone, but every once in awhile the humps of their backs would appear above the water's surface. Whenever this happened, the people felt it was a bad omen: the crops were going to fail that year or there would be a shortage of grazing grass.

Those who do not believe in the serpents say that it is only superstition: what the people are seeing is a trail of floating foam. These unbelievers often mention a priest who rowed across the water, passing directly over the spot where the serpents live. His successful crossing proves that there is nothing to fear.

Based on Jón Árnason I, 635–636

FIVE

Magicians

Sæmundur and the Black School

Once upon a time, somewhere in the world, there was a Black School where students learned witchcraft and ancient mystical arts. Because the school was hidden deep underground, the students lived without fresh air or sunlight and studied in pitch-black rooms—hence the name.

There were no teachers at the Black School. Every student learned on their own, reading from books with fiery letters that made them easily seen in the dark. For meals, a hairy gray hand would push through a wall and present each student with their food and drink. When the meal was finished, the hand gathered up the cups and plates and disappeared.

The students stayed at the Black School for five to seven years, always leaving on the exact day and hour that they had arrived. When a student left the school, he was fully trained, with all the skills necessary to practice the magician's craft.

On the students' final day each year, there was a massive scramble to get out of school. Everyone knew that the Master retained the right to keep for himself the last magician to leave the building. Since the school's Master was the Devil himself, no one wanted to be the last one out and spend eternity serving him.

One year, three Icelanders named Sæmundur the Learned, Kálfur Árnason, and Hálfdán Eldjárnsson were about to leave the Black School. The young men had arrived on the same day and were now scheduled to leave at exactly the same time. Years earlier, Sæmundur had told his friends that he was willing to be the last student to leave the school when their years of study were finished. The other two magicians were delighted.

What they didn't know was that one night while sleeping, Sæmundur had been visited by Bogi Einasson. Bogi entered Sæmundur's dream and said, "You are a foolish man! You enter this school, forget about your God, and turn your heart over to witchcraft. If you expect to have a future, leave this place immediately."

"I cannot," Sæmundur replied. "No one is allowed to leave the school."

"See what a fool you are?" said Bogi. "You entered a school that now holds you captive. But if you are willing, I will tell you how to safely leave."

"You know everything, Bogi," Sæmundur said. "Your wisdom makes the rest of us seem like children. I'll accept your help. Tell me how."

"As you prepare to leave the school, toss a cloak over your shoulders, but do not fasten it," said Bogi. "When you approach the exit, the Devil will try to grab you. Slip out of the cloak and run as quickly as possible through the door. Even though you will be free from the school, you will still have to contend with the Master. He will miss you the moment that you are gone and begin to search for you.

"When you are a safe distance away, remove your right shoe and fill it with blood. Carry the shoe on your head for the rest of the day. In the evening, the Master will gaze up at the stars, whose movements and positions he is skilled at reading and see a bloody halo around your star. He will believe that you are dead.

"While travelling the next day, fill your shoe with

salt and water and carry it on your head. The Master will not bother you during the day, but that night, he will again examine the stars looking for you. He will see a watery halo around your star and think that you died by drowning in the sea.

"On the third day, open a vein in your side and let the blood trickle into your shoe. Mix the blood with soil and carry the shoe on your head for the entire day. In the evening, the Master will look to the stars and see an earthy blood-stained halo and think that you are not only dead, but buried.

"Afterward, the Master will discover that you are alive and be amazed by your cleverness. He will take pride in the thought that you learned your skills and wisdom at his school. He will stop pursuing you and wish you well."

Bogi finished his advice to Sæmundur and left the dream.

On the day Sæmundur was scheduled to leave the Black School, he threw a cloak over his shoulders, leaving the fastenings open. At the staircase that led to the upper world, the Devil grabbed him and triumphantly said, "You belong to me!"

Sæmundur slipped out of the cloak and ran full speed up the stairs, leaving the Devil standing with an empty garment in his hand. The moment he crossed the threshold of the heavy iron door, it slammed shut behind him and bruised the backs of his heels.

Some stories say that when Sæmundur entered the doorway to the outside world, the sun shone on him and threw his shadow onto the opposite wall. As the Devil stretched out his hand to grab him again, Sæmundur called out, "I am not the last person. Look, someone is following me!"

The Devil spun around and grabbed the shadow, mistaking it for a man. Sæmundur escaped, but from that moment on, he lived without a shadow. For whatever the Devil takes, he never returns.

In any case, Sæmundur escaped from the school and the clutches of the Devil. He followed all of Bogi's advice as he and his companions, Kálfur and Hálfdán, travelled toward home. Along the way they learned that the parish at Oddi was looking for a priest. The three men rushed to the king and each man asked to be granted the position. The king, knowing that he was dealing with powerful magicians, promised the job to whichever man reached Oddi first.

Sæmundur immediately called for the Devil. "I need to get to Iceland as quickly as possible," he said. "Will you swim across the ocean and let me ride on your back? If I arrive on shore and the hem of my coat is dry, I will become your slave."

The devil agreed. He changed into a seal and Sæmundur climbed onto his back. Together, they journeyed across the open sea. Much to the Devil's dismay, Sæmundur amused himself along the way by reading from the Psalms of David in the Holy Book.

Once Iceland loomed large on the horizon, Sæmundur closed his book and used it to bash the seal in the head. He hit the animal so hard that it sank beneath the water. Sæmundur swam to shore, and because his coat was wet, the Devil lost their bargain. Sæmundur quickly won the race and became the priest at Oddi.

Before he left for Iceland, Sæmundur had promised to marry a witch from Saxony. When he had not returned for her, the witch realized that he had played her for a fool and she plotted her revenge.

Several years passed before the witch decided to

send Sæmundur a gift of a golden chest. She ordered that no one should open it but him. The chest travelled across the ocean to Iceland and reached a southern harbor. The crew of the ship immediately sent the chest to Oddi. It reached Sæmundur while he was in his church. The gift came as no surprise to the priest. He welcomed the messenger and told him to place the chest on the altar.

The chest sat on the altar all night. The next morning, Sæmundur carried it to the top of Mount Hekla and threw it into a gulley. The chest landed at the bottom, and from that moment on the volcanic fires of Hekla have burned regularly.

Sæmundur often reminded his people that each day there was a wishing hour. It happened in the wink of an eye and few people ever succeeded in catching it.

One day while sitting with the maidservants, he said, "Girls, this is the wishing hour. Make a wish!"

Without hesitating, a servant girl named Gudrún cried out,

> A single wish, no more no less,
> Is now my heart's desire:
> That seven sons I may possess,
> And Sæmundur be their sire.

Angry at hearing the girl's wish, Sæmundur said, "And you will die while giving birth to the last of them!"

Gudrún married Sæmundur and was very proud of her new position as the wife of a priest and magician. So proud that once, when a poor man came to her and asked for a drink, she said, "Go to the river, my good man. The bishop's horse must do the same!"

Sæmundur kept the clothes that Gudrún had worn

when she was a servant girl, showing them to her from time to time, trying to keep her pride in check. Gudrún gave Sæmundur the seven sons she had wished for, but as he predicted, while delivering the last boy, she died.

One time Sæmundur's old friend Kálfur Árnason came to him with a problem. While they were still at the Black School, Kálfur had promised to give himself to the Devil when he died. Now that he was back in Iceland, he didn't want to fulfill that promise. He asked Sæmundur if he knew of a way to escape from his dilemma.

Sæmundur said, "Let one of your bull calves live and name him Árni. When he is old enough, he will sire another calf that you must name Kálfur. By doing this, there will be another Kálfur Árnason to give to the devil."

Kálfur was delighted with this idea and took his friend's advice.

Some time later, the Devil arrived and asked him to fulfill his promise. The Devil said, "I want my Kálfur Árnason!"

"I will give him to you," said Kálfur. "I have no objection to your request."

Kálfur walked out to the field and fetched the second calf. He presented it to the Devil and said, "Here is your Kálfur Árnason."

The Devil could not deny the truth of his words. He had been made to play the fool. Luckily for the calf, the Devil allowed him to live to an old age and die a natural death.

The Devil and Sæmundur battled many times over the years. From their first encounter at the Black School, the Devil tried to take his revenge on the magician, but each time Sæmundur beat him at his own game.

One day the Devil turned himself into a fly. He hid under the skin on the milk in Sæmundur's bowl, hoping to slide into his stomach and kill him. When Sæmundur lifted the bowl to his lips, he saw the wiggling fly. He wrapped the milk skin around the insect and put it into a bag.

He placed the bag on the altar in his church and forced the fly to stay there until he finished his next Mass, which he deliberately allowed to drag on and on. When the service was finally over, he opened the bag and set the Devil free. It can be said with confidence that the Devil never had a less enjoyable day in all his existence.

Sæmundur the Learned died in 1133. He rests on the northwest side of St. Nicholas Church at Oddi. The stone that marks his grave is made of uncut rock. Some people say that after three days in the grave, he rose up and began reciting one of the ancient poems he had included in his Edda. (That collection of ancient northern poems of pagan gods and early heroes was once thought to have been written by Sæmundur.)

Others believe that if sick people watch the gravestone at night, their illnesses will disappear.

Based on Jón Árnason I, 471, 475–478, 484, 480–481, 486–487

The Witch Ride

In his introduction to tales about witchcraft, Jón Árnason reveals the secret to soaring through the air safely—a witch-ride bridle. They are fairly easy to make. First, dig up a newly-buried corpse and tear off a strip of skin along the entire length of the spine. This you will use for the reins. Next, remove the dead person's scalp; this is the head piece of the bridle. They take the jaw bone for your bit and the hip bones for the cheek pieces. Assemble all the parts, chant a spell over the bridle, and it will be ready to use. Place your bridle on any man or beast, piece of wood or bit of stone. Sit on the object you choose and it will rise up into the air and fly quicker than lightening wherever you tell it to go.

Now to our story.

A wealthy young pastor had just married a beautiful young woman. He was devoted to his new bride and she soon became an example of the perfect wife for all the women of his parish—and the neighboring parishes as well.

However, she had one flaw that greatly concerned her husband. Every Christmas Eve, she disappeared for the entire night and refused to tell anyone where she had gone. It was the only time they argued. Her husband was concerned and begged her to reveal her secret to him. Her reply was always the same—where she went was none of his business.

One day a young drifter was hired to work at the parsonage. Although he seemed rather small and weak, everyone agreed that he worked hard and seemed smarter than most of the men.

Christmas Eve came again. The youth was in the stable grooming the pastor's horse when suddenly his mistress, the pastor's wife, appeared at his side. She seemed to be in a hurry, but willingly engaged him in polite conversation. Then the next thing he knew, she had pulled a bridle out from under her apron and put it on his head. Because the bridle was magical, the youth could not resist.

The mistress climbed onto his back, and as if he were a winged creature, they flew into the night. Skimming above the mountains and valleys, crossing over the rivers and sea, they at last landed outside a tiny house. The pastor's wife tethered the youth to a hook, approached the door, and knocked. A man opened it and greeted her warmly, gently ushering her inside.

After they disappeared into the house, the youth struggled to loosen the bridle from the hook. Once he succeeded, he removed it from his head and shoved it into his coat pocket. Then he climbed onto the roof of the house and, peeking through a crack, watched what was happening inside.

The man who answered the door was sitting at the head of a table. Twelve women surrounded him, respectfully listening to his every word. Then one by one the women recounted for the master their various spells and magical accomplishments. When the pastor's wife spoke, she proudly announced that she had ridden to the house on a living boy. The master was very impressed. He said that to ride a human was the most powerful of witch-rides. He told her that her magical power surpassed all the other witches. He said to her, "I know of nobody, besides myself, who can make a human fly."

The other women were eager to learn this new skill. The master laid a gray book onto the table. It was inscribed with fiery letters that shone throughout the room. He began to teach the women from the book, explaining the details of its contents to them.

The youth listened carefully and committed everything that he heard to memory. When the lesson was over, each woman brought out a bottle of red liquid. With great reverence, they handed them to the master and he sipped from each one. When this ritual was finished, the witches left the house.

Peeking over the edge of the roof, the youth watched as each witch grabbed their own bridle and mounted an object. One rode the leg bone of a horse, another a jawbone, and a third a shoulder bone and so on. They all rose into the air and flew away.

When the pastor's wife realized that her mount was missing and rushed all around the house searching for the boy. When her attention was elsewhere, the youth leaped down from the roof and threw the bridle over her head. He jumped onto her back and ordered her to fly. By listening to what the master had taught, he skillfully guided the pastor's wife back to the stable.

The youth dismounted and tied the witch in one of the stalls. He ran to the farmhouse and told the entire household his story. Everyone was amazed, especially the poor young pastor. He questioned his wife and in the end, she confessed that she and eleven other pastor's wives had spent several years at the Black School. The Devil had taught them their craft and she had only one year left of her studies. For his fee, the Devil required their blood, which is what was in the bottles that the youth saw him drink.

In time, the pastor's wife received a fitting punishment for her crimes.

Based on Jón Árnason, I, 426–428

Loftur the Enchanter

Once there was a young man named Loftur who attended the school at Hólar in the north of Iceland. He studied the art of magic and was often the instigator when his fellow students played tricks on one another.

One Christmas, he decided to go home and visit his parents. He cast a spell on a servant girl, placed a witch-ride bridle in her mouth, and rode her like a horse to and from his parents' house.

When they returned to the school, the girl was in so much pain that she took to her bed and stayed there for several days. She never spoke of her experience to anyone and remained silent about it for as long as Loftur lived.

Another time, Loftur learned that a servant girl was pregnant with his child. One of her duties was to take a large trough-shaped pan and use it to clean out the ashes from the fire and carry them outside. One day, as she was struggling under the heavy burden, Loftur decided to ease her workload by opening a passage through one of the walls. The girl stepped into the opening, but then became frightened and hesitated. That hesitation lasted just long enough for the magic spell to end and the wall to close around her.

Years later, when the wall was torn down, workers discovered the girl's skeleton. She was standing upright and they could see the unborn baby's skeleton and her last load of ashes.

The dean of the school and pastor of the cathedral, Thorleifur Skaftason, rebuked Loftur for his behavior toward the servant girls. Unfortunately, this chastizing didn't faze the young magician. Nor did it stop the bad behavior.

Some time later, Loftur and the dean quarreled bitterly. But since the dean was a great man of God and understood the art of magic, Loftur was powerless to harm him.

Determined to be a great sorcerer, Loftur studied hard and memorized everything the famous Grayskin book of magic had to teach. Toward the end of his studies, he consulted several great sorcerers and was pleased to learn that he knew everything that they did. Loftur's obsession for knowledge made him so strange and ill-tempered that even his classmates were afraid of him. Not one of them dared to challenge or contradict him, even when they were horrified by his actions.

Early one winter, Loftur approached a young lad and asked him to help summon the spirits of several bishops who lived in ancient times. The boy was reluctant, but when Loftur threatened to kill him, he agreed. Loftur told the boy that he wanted him to climb up the bell tower and hold onto the bell rope. He must stand perfectly still, watch Loftur's every move, and at his signal, immediately ring the bell.

"Here is my plan," said Loftur. "You see, people like me, who study the art of magic, can only use it for evil purposes. When we die, we are sent directly to hell and into the clutches of the Devil. But if a magician has enough knowledge, the Devil has no power over him. Just as he did for Sæmundur the Learned, the Devil would have to serve the magician and never receive anything in return. With that much knowledge, a man can then decide for himself whether he wants to use his power for good or for evil.

"It is impossible to obtain that amount of knowledge. Not since the Black School closed and Bishop Gottskálk the Cruel ordered his people to bury him with his Redskin book of sorcery has anyone accomplished it.

"My plan is to summon Bishop Gottskálk's spirit and force him to give me that book. Once I have his powerful spells, all the other ancient bishops that I summon will be powerless against me. I will force them to perform their magic and reveal to me all that they learned during their lifetimes. Unfortunately, I can only summon ancient bishops because those who lived in later years are buried with the Holy Scriptures resting on their chests.

"My present and eternal well-being depends on you faithfully doing what I tell you. Make sure that you ring the bell at the moment I give you the signal, neither too soon nor too late. I will reward you if we succeed."

The two agreed on a signal and discussed the final details of Loftur's plan. When everyone else was in bed, Loftur and the boy went to the church. A bright moon illuminated the inside of the building as the boy took his place in the tower. Loftur climbed into the pulpit and began to cast his spell. Suddenly, a man with a kind but solemn face rose out of the ground. He wore a crown on his head and appeared to be one of the earliest bishops.

The dead bishop said to Loftur, "Stop, you wretched man, while there is still time. If you disturb the sleep of my brother Gvendur (also known as Guðmundur the Good), he will curse you."

Loftur ignored the bishop and continued to summon the others. One by one they appeared from their graves in the order in which they lived. Each bishop wore a white gown with a cross hanging around his neck. Carrying staffs in their hands, they each walked up to Loftur and exchanged a few words. Three of the bishops wore crowns on their heads, which, according to Icelandic tradition, meant that they had been saints. None of the three revealed any magical knowledge to Loftur.

Bishop Gottskálk tried to resist Loftur's spell to summon him. The three crowned bishops tried to help Gottskálk. They stood with their hands lifted high and their faces turned toward Loftur. The other bishops remained silent, standing with their backs to him.

Loftur ignored them all and focused his energy on the one resistant bishop. He began reading the psalms of penance backward, reciting them in the Devil's name.

Suddenly, there was a loud crash and Gottskálk appeared. He wore no cross around his neck but held a staff in his left hand and a red book under his right arm. He glared at the assembled group of bishops. Then he turned to Loftur, who was concentrating on his spell and moving closer. He grinned at Loftur and said, "Great spell, my son! Much better than I expected. But you cannot have the Redskin book."

Loftur became like a man possessed. He chanted and chanted—harder and harder. In a final effort to make Gottskálk turn over the book, Loftur recited the words of the Benediction and the Lord's Prayer backwards, calling them out in the name of the Devil.

Suddenly, the entire church heaved and shook. The boy in the tower nearly fainted with fright as he watched Loftur stretch out his hand for the book. Thinking that this was his signal, the boy yanked on the bell rope. The bell tolled and with a mighty roar, all the bishops vanished!

Loftur stood speechless, and then slowly rested his head in his hands.

A short while later, he walked over to the boy and said, "Things did not go as I had planned. It is my fault. If only I had waited until dawn, I could have denied Bishop Gottskálk refuge in his grave and he would have freely surrendered the book to me.

"But when I saw the book and heard his taunt, I was consumed with anger. I was determined to cast a spell that would force him to release it to me. Then I realized what I was doing. With only one more spell, the entire church would have sunk into the ground.

"And that is exactly what Gottskálk had intended all along. In that final moment, I saw the faces of the crowned bishops and was terrified, even knowing that you were there to ring the bell. The book was so close—I thought I could get it. I touched the corner... it was so close... I thought I could grab it... keep it from falling.

"Ah! What is to be, will be. My fate is sealed. You will receive your reward, but must never speak of this matter to anyone."

From that night on, Loftur rarely spoke and began to lose his mind. He feared being left alone and each night as darkness fell, he insisted that someone light every lamp. He was often heard to mutter, "On the third Sunday of Lent I will suffer the torments of Hell."

In desperation, Loftur sought refuge with a pastor who lived at Stadarstad. It was said that this pastor could relieve the burdens of those who were troubled and free them of sorcery just by placing his hand on them. When Loftur begged pastor for shelter, the godly man took pity on the disturbed magician and allowed him into his home.

Day and night, the faithful pastor never left Loftur's side. Loftur slowly recovered his sanity, but the pastor still feared for his eternal soul. Although Loftur accompanied him on his visits to the sick and suffering, he never saw Loftur pray.

Time passed and the evening before the third Sunday of Lent arrived. Loftur was sick and the pastor sat near him, trying to comfort him.

Early the next morning, a messenger arrived with word that a close friend of the pastor and a member of his parish was at death's door. This man begged the pastor to come quickly and administer the last rites and prepare him for death.

The pastor could not deny his friend's request. He asked Loftur if he was well enough to go along, but Loftur said no, the pain and weakness made it too difficult for him to move. The pastor assured Loftur that he would be safe if he stayed in the house. Then he blessed him and gave him a parting kiss.

At the door of the house, the pastor fell to his knees and prayed. While making the sign of the cross over the threshold, he whispered, "God alone knows if this man can be saved. Perhaps there are stronger prayers than mine directed against him."

The pastor travelled to his friend's home, ministered to his needs, and was beside him when he died.

Soon after the pastor left the house, Loftur's health rapidly improved. Noticing that it was a beautiful day, he decided to walk outside. The men of the house were down at the fishing huts and the women and children were powerless to stop him.

Loftur left the house and travelled to a neighboring farm. He met an elderly farmer, reputed to be something of a rogue, returning from a fishing trip. Loftur begged him to launch his boat and row out a short way so they could fish. Since the older man was always interested in a bit of fishing for fun, he agreed.

Later, a man who was standing on the shore reported that he saw their boat floating out to sea. He swore that a hairy gray arm reached out of the water, grabbed the boat, and dragged it, along with the two men, under the water. Although the sea remained calm all day, no one ever saw either of them again.

Based on Jón Árnason I, 572–575

Thorgeir's Bull

It was autumn when a man named Thorgeir the Wizard travelled on a fishing boat with his brother Stefan and their uncle Andres. As the men fished off the coast of the island of Hrísey, they decided to have some fun and create a supernatural bull.

Thorgeir purchased a newborn calf from a woman on the island. He killed it and carefully skinned the animal, from head to hoof, so that the hide came off in one big piece. Then the three men cast a spell on the carcass and brought it back to life.

Not satisfied with an ordinary living carcass, they decided to gather together eight different personalities or spirit forces from the natural world and put them into their bull. These spirit forces came from a bird, a dog, a cat, a mouse, a man, two sea animals, and the air. When they were finished, the bull had nine different spirit forces living inside him, the ninth being his own cattle spirit. Having these different spirit forces allowed the bull to travel easily through the air, across the land, and deep under the sea. They also allowed him to change his appearance into any one of the nine.

Still not completely satisfied with the bull and determined to make him impervious to any magical force, Thorgeir took the afterbirth of a newborn child and threw it over the bull.

Finally, the men were satisfied with their creation.

In acknowledgement of all Thorgeir's hard work, they named the frightening animal Thorgeir's Bull.

Thorgeir became the first of the three men to use the bull. He proposed to a girl named Gudrún Bessadóttir, and when she refused his offer, he sent the bull to attack her. Although the animal didn't kill Gudrún, he tormented her and forced her to live in constant fear. Eventually, six to eight strong men had to accompany her whenever she travelled from farm to farm. No one felt safe when they were alone with Gudrún because she never knew when the bull would attack. Sometimes her journeys were peaceful, but at other times, the bull snatched her from the back of her horse and flung her fifteen or twenty feet away.

One time, while attending a church service, the bull began to torment and beat Gudrún. When he left the building, she was lying helpless on the ground, with pain shooting through her entire body. A man from the church decided to follow the bull. He found the animal lying on the sloping roof of a nearby farmhouse with his head was hanging over the peak. The man could clearly see up the bull's nostrils, and to his surprise, saw a gray string stretching from the bull to the church. But before he could investigate further, the bull disappeared.

Not long after this event, Gudrún died.

Gudrún's death did not satisfy the bull so he turned his attention toward a close relative of hers named Helga. The bull found Helga living on the Sund farm in Höfdahverfi with her husband Magnús. He began to unceasingly torment her.

Now, living near Helga's farm was a magician named Torfi. The people of the neighborhood begged him to destroy the bull and free the tormented Helga. When Torfi arrived at the Sund farm, he found the bull in the middle of their living room, happily sitting on top of Helga.

While Helga complained about the weight that was pressing down on her bare feet, Torfi tried to destroy the bull. Unfortunately, he soon discovered that the bull was protected by the afterbirth, a powerful symbol of good fortune. He told the unhappy couple that since he could not tell whether the afterbirth was taken off the child from head to toe or from toe to head, no spell would work. As long as the bull had the afterbirth, it could not be defeated.

Before long, Helga also died and for a while, the bull continued to torture her family.

Thorgeir's plan to use the bull to destroy Gudrún succeeded, and soon he was commanding the animal to torture any person who angered him. Sometimes, just for fun, he would send the bull into a herd of cows, causing them to stampede and scatter across the countryside. The bull so frightened Thorgeir's neighbors that before long, they thought they heard the animal's bellow whenever they ventured out at night or into a dense fog.

On one occasion, Thorgeir walked to Hallgilsstadir for an evening prayer meeting. While waiting for it to start, he stood outside, staring into a clear bright sky. When the master of the house came to tell him that the meeting was about to begin, a huge bank of fog started to roll over the northern mountains.

"To the Devil with him," Thorgeir said. "He'll travel no further today!"

A short time later, a violent snowstorm descended on the farm. The people at the meeting thought that Thorgeir had been talking about the bull, since one of its spirits was air and the storm had obeyed his command.

Although the bull was devoted to Thorgeir, he could also cause trouble for him. Whenever Thorgeir's Bull was unable to carry out a command, he would return to his master and try to kill him. Thorgeir was a talented wizard, but as time wore on, it became more and more difficult to defend himself against his own creation. He used every spell he knew to escape the determined bull.

On one occasion, the bull made an all-out effort to kill his master. Thorgeir tried everything he could think of, but was soon forced to seek refuge in the house with his wife and child. In the midst of this crisis, Thorgeir wanted to offer his child to the bull. His wife clutched the baby to her chest and begging him not to make such a horrid sacrifice. She suggested that he offer a heifer instead. Thorgeir went to the barn, released the heifer, and an hour later found it torn into little pieces not far from their farmhouse.

Eventually the bull stopped trying to kill his master, but continued to torment other members of his family. Thorgeir became so frightened of his creation that he never allowed his daughters to go anywhere without a runic charm in their apron pocket to protect them from the beast.

Thorgeir died in 1803 at the age of 83. He never destroyed his bull and some say that while lying on his deathbed, at the moment he breathed his last, a gray cat crouched on his chest—a cat, one of the spirit forms of the bull.

The bull took on many different shapes. Sometimes he looked like a man or dog, but most often he stayed in the form of a horned bull, dragging his bloody hide behind him. Whatever shape he embodied, he was ugly enough to terrify anyone who saw him.

Based on Jón Árnason I, 336–338

Eiríkur of Vogsós

There once lived an old man in the Biskupstunga district who knew many ancient stories. He lived alone, but had two cherished possessions: a heifer that he lovingly cared for and a book whose contents no one ever read. Before the old man died, he told the priest to bury him with his cow and book. He warned the priest that if his instructions were not carried out, there would be trouble throughout the parish.

Many years after the old man died, a lad named Eiríkur Magnússon (later called Eiríkur of Vogsós) and a few of his friends raised the old man's spirit and forced him to give them part of the book. From those pages, they composed a tome of magic called the Grayskin.

For years, the book sat on a table in the school-house at Skálholt. When word reached the bishop of of this town that Eiríkur of Vogsós practiced magic, he ordered Eiríkur to appear before him. He showed the wizard the Grayskin book and asked if he could understand anything that was written on the pages. Eiríkur studied the script and then said to the bishop, "I can't read a word of it." He swore an oath that he did not understand what was written in the book and returned home.

Later, Eiríkur told a friend that he had lied. He recognized every letter, except one, that was written on the pages of the Grayskin book. He begged his friend to wait until after he was dead before revealing his secret.

With his name renowned throughout the country, young men travelled great distances in search of Eiríkur of Vogsós. They pleaded with him to teach them his magical spells. Soon there were so many petitioners that Eiríkur was forced to test each man and separate the good students from the bad ones. If he found a man worthy of his instruction, he accepted the youth as an apprentice and taught him everything he knew.

One time an enthusiastic lad caught Eiríkur's attention. He said to the boy, "Stay with me until Sunday and we'll travel to Krysuvík. At the end of the journey I will tell you whether or not I will be your teacher."

On Sunday morning they left Eiríkur's house, travelling toward Krysuvík. When they reached the sand flats, Eiríkur turned to the boy and said, "I forgot my handbook! Please fetch it for me, but be sure that you do not open it."

The boy rode to Eiríkur's house, found the book under his pillow, and started the journey back. Along the way, curiosity got the better of him and he opened the book. Immediately, he was surrounded by a host of devils. They cried out in unison, "What should we do? What should we do?"

The boy quickly answered, "Braid ropes from the sand." And the devils immediately fell to the ground and set to work.

The lad rode on, catching up with Eiríkur in a lava field. He handed him the book and Eiríkur said, "You opened it."

"No," the boy lied. "I did not."

On their return trip, Eiríkur spotted a group of devils sitting on the sand trying to braid it into rope. "Even though you denied it, I knew you opened my book," he said to the boy. "But I see that you kept your composure and cleverly handled the devils. It will be worth my while to teach you."

The boy remained with Eiríkur and proved to be a worthy pupil. As for the devils? No one knows how long they continued at their ridiculous task.

Another time, two men tracked down Eiríkur and asked him to teach them the magical arts. With a look of amazement, Eiríkur told the men that they were misinformed—he didn't know any magic. But since they had travelled such a long distance, they were welcome to spend the night at his house. The men gladly accepted his offer, ate a hearty supper, and slept soundly through the night.

The next morning, Eiríkur suggested a leisurely ride around the farm to inspect his fields and herds. A short distance from the house, they encountered an old woman carrying an infant in her arms. She approached Eiríkur and started begging him to help her feed the child.

Eiríkur looked down on the pitiful woman and said with an angry voice, "I will do nothing of the sort!" He tried to ride around her, but she grabbed his horse's bridle and cried louder, pleading with him for mercy. She told him that she was a widow, without a home, food, or money.

As her pleas continued, Eiríkur grew angrier and said, "Stop whining! This world would be a better place if someone killed you and all the beggars like you—troublesome, wretched people!"

No matter how hard he tried to escape, the old woman continued to weep and cling to his horse's bridle. In desperation, Eiríkur turned to his guests and said, "If one of you will kill this old hag, I will teach you my magic."

The first man stared at him in amazement. "I am surprised that the great Eiríkur is such an ungodly man," he said. "No matter what you offer, I would never commit such a heinous crime."

"I see no harm in it," said the second man. "If Eiríkur requests it, I will kill the witch. It is a good thing to rid the country of such people. They ought to thank me for ending their wretched lives." He turned his horse toward the woman and she immediately disappeared.

"Ah, ha!" said Eiríkur, turning toward the second man. "You may continue your journey. I would never teach such a heartless fellow!" He smiled at the first young man and told him that he was welcome to stay and become one of his pupils.

Some time later a group of men, travelling from the market, were forced to stop on the bank of a river. The tide was in and the water was too deep for the horses to safely cross. Eiríkur approached the travellers and asked for a drink. Every man refused him except one. That man willingly took out his flask and offered it to Eiríkur.

"Unload your horses near the mouth of the river," Eiríkur said to the kind stranger. "Take your time, but do not remove their saddles. When the others have unsaddled and hobbled their horses, quickly reload your animals and I will help you safely across the water."

The man followed Eiríkur's instructions. When he was finished reloading his horses, Eiríkur reappeared and led them downriver to where a bridge of snow crossed the estuary. Although the snow seemed thin, Eiríkur promised the man that it was safe.

The other travellers watched in amazement as they crossed the water. They quickly rounded up their horses, loaded them and raced toward the snow bridge.

When they arrived, the bridge was gone and the water was again impassable. Disappointed, the men returned to their campsite, unloaded and hobbled the horses, set up their tents, and settled in for the night.

Eiríkur tricked the men because he knew that each one had refused him a drink out of meanness, not because their flasks were empty.

Another time, a very sad traveller arrived at Vogsós. Eiríkur pulled him aside and asked what was bothering him. At first the man was reluctant to reveal his problem, but with Eiríkur's gentle prodding, he admitted that he was sad because his betrothed had recently rejected him. He asked if Eiríkur could help, but the magician told him that he could not.

The rejected man climbed into bed and was soon fast asleep. Eiríkur remained awake, patiently waiting. In the middle of the night, he was rewarded with a knock on the door. He opened the door and standing outside, dressed in a petticoat and soaked to the skin, was a shivering young woman. She greeted Eiríkur and begged for shelter for the night.

Inviting her inside, Eiríkur guided her toward the warm fire and covered her with a blanket. Once she was seated, he asked her why she was out on such a cold night without proper clothing.

"Earlier this evening," she said. "I went outside to collect the laundry. It started to rain. I ran to where it usually hangs, but somehow I lost my way in the dark and ended up here."

"I'm glad you are safe," said Eiríkur. "But we have a problem. My house is full. There is no place for you to sleep unless you are willing to share a bed with that man in the corner." He pointed toward where his sad guest lay, quiet and still.

The girl told Eiríkur that she was willing to sleep with anyone, rather than die from the cold. She climbed into the warm bed and immediately recognized who was beside her. The couple talked long into the night and by morning were reunited. Eventually they married and lived out the rest of their lives in wedded bliss.

Time passed, and the bishop from Skálholt, after hearing many stories about Eiríkur and his practice of witchcraft, piously decided that Eiríkur was no longer a godly man and must be stripped of his priesthood. He sent eighteen students to publicly remove Eiríkur's robes and announce that he was unfit for his office. The men were proud of their mission and as they rode along, each one bragged about how they were going to force the evil Eiríkur out into the streets.

One morning, Eiríkur woke early and left his house. A short time later, he returned, groaning in pain and sorrow. He ordered his servants to keep all the animals close to the barn. A storm was approaching and it was dangerous to release them into the pastures. When the blizzard descended on the area, it snowed so heavily that a man, crossing from one part of the farm to another, could scarcely stand and was knocked about by the high winds and deep drifting snow.

Shortly after midday, there was a knock on the farmhouse door. Eiríkur opened it, and standing outside was one of the bishop's men. Eiríkur invited him inside. Throughout the day, one by one, the eighteen men who had lost their way in the snowstorm arrived at Eiríkur's house. Eiríkur treated each man with kindness, offering him dry clothing and a warm stable for his horse. He was the perfect host.

By morning, the men were so fond of him that they refused to carry out the bishop's orders. They returned to Skálholt and told the bishop what they had done. He was so furious that he vowed to travel personally to Vogsós and perform the task.

Spring passed quickly and when summer arrived, the bishop and his entourage travelled to Vogsós. They set up camp near where Eiríkur lived. Since it was a weekday, the bishop decided to wait until Sunday to strip the priest of his gowns. After warning his men to stay away from Eiríkur and not accept anything he might offer them, the bishop summoned Eiríkur to appear before him.

Eiríkur arrived at the bishop's tent in a merry mood. The bishop was confused by this lack of concern over the seriousness of the situation and did not know how to respond. Instead of condemning the priest, he asked for a tour of his church. Eiríkur gladly escorted him through the buildings and to the bishop's amazement, everything was in perfect order.

While the bishop continued his inspection, one of his servants walked to the farmhouse for hot coals to build a fire. As the servant passed by the porch, Eiríkur called out a greeting. He pulled a bottle of wine from his pocket and offered the man a drink.

"I can't take any," said the servant. "Bishop's orders."

Eiríkur laughed and pointed out to him that it was only wine; what harm could come from drinking it. The man politely refused again, but Eiríkur continued to pressure him. Finally, the servant gave in and accepted the flask. He took one sip and was so surprised by its delightful flavor that he consumed the entire bottle. When he was finished, he asked Eiríkur for another bottle so that he could give some to the bishop with his evening meal. Silently laughing at his success, Eiríkur handed the man a second bottle and watched him shove it into his pocket.

The bishop finished his tour of the church and returned to his tent. At supper that evening, the servant poured him a glass of wine. No sooner had the sweet drink touched his lips than he changed his mind about casting Eiríkur out of the church.

After finishing his meal, the bishop went to Eiríkur's house and decided to stay for the rest of the week. His visit was so enjoyable that when he returned to Skálholt he never threatened Eiríkur's position in the church again. In fact, the bishop spent the rest of his days praising Eiríkur and everything that he did.

One day a package arrived at Vogsós. It contained a woolen sweater, a gift for Eiríkur from a woman named Thordís. Thordís was a proud member of the Stokkseyri community, the granddaughter of a sheriff and the niece of a historian to the king of Denmark. Known for her unreasonable treatment of those around her, she sent the red trimmed, bright blue sweater with specific instructions that Eiríkur wear it when he conducted Mass at Krysuvik.

One frosty Sunday, Eiríkur decided to wear the sweater. He put it on, mounted his horse, and headed toward the church. Suddenly, the sweater began to shrink. It wrapped so tightly around his body that his face swelled and turned blue. Eiríkur fell off his horse, unable to call for help. With foam bubbling out of his mouth, he watched in agony and hope as a small boy approached him, saw his predicament, and quickly cut off the sweater.

Eiríkur thanked the boy for saving his life, then immediately rode home and locked the sweater in a chest. In response to Thordís's kind gift, he spun some gray yarn and knitted it into a petticoat. He sent his present to Thordís, who was delighted with its thickness and warmth.

Winter arrived and one evening Eiríkur ordered that every door to the house be tightly locked. He said that they were to remain closed, even if someone knocked. No one in the household was bothered by this request since they had just survived a fierce snowstorm and were now facing freezing cold temperatures. Surely no sane person would be out in such wicked weather.

Later that night, to everyone's surprise, there was a knock on the door. Those lying nearest to Eiríkur heard him say, "Whoever is at the door, let them knock a second time."

The knocking grew louder and more insistent, but the priest still refused to get out of bed. When the stranger knocked for the third time, it was weak and soft. Eiríkur threw back his covers and slowly dressed and walked to the door. When he opened it, there stood Thordís, the woman who knitted him the sweater, with a chamber pot stuck in her hands. Nearly dead from the cold, she was wearing only a chemise and the petticoat that Eiríkur knitted for her.

Eiríkur greeted her with a smile and said, "My dear, why are you out in such awful weather? Your errand must be an urgent one."

He invited her inside, and when she was a bit warmer, she said, "I went outside to empty my chamber pot and a violent storm blew in. It suddenly got so dark that I lost my way. I've been wandering around all night." She lifted the chamber pot and said, "And for some reason, I can't seem to drop this pot!"

"That reminds me," said Eiríkur. "I never thanked you for the beautiful sweater. It was more than I deserved. I returned your kindness by causing the storm and making you lose your way. Your night in the bitter cold should be a reminder to never play tricks on Eiríkur of Vogsós."

The two friends laughed over the incidents and when Thordís recovered, she happily returned home.

When Eiríkur was close to death, he called for his coffin bearers. They stood around his bed and listened to his warning. He said that a violent hailstorm would hinder their progress as they carried his coffin to the church. No matter how strong the wind or how big the hail stones, his coffin must not touch the ground from the moment they picked it up until it was safely inside the church. When they entered the building, the hailstorm would stop.

Once inside, they would see two birds, a white one and a black one, viciously fighting. If the white bird won and settled in the church rafters, they were to bury him in the churchyard. If the black bird won and settled in the rafters, his soul was lost and they must bury him outside the churchyard.

Eiríkur died and everything happened as he predicted. In the end, the white bird was victorious over the black bird and, to everyone's relief, Eiríkur was buried in holy ground.

Based on Jón Árnason I, 543–546, 550, 552–555, 565

Hálfdán and Björn the Fiddler

Hálfdán was a priest whose widowed sister Hildigunnur and her son Björn lived in poverty. Björn was a strong young man, but his love for playing the fiddle meant that he spent very little time at home helping his mother. He preferred to wander from farm to farm and parish to parish entertaining anyone who would listen. Frustrated with the boy, Hildigunnur finally decided to send the lad to his uncle Hálfdán with a message begging him to find the boy some useful work.

One fine day, Hildigunnur handed Björn a bag of food and a new pair of shoes. She ushered him out the door and told him to go straight to his uncle's house. Along the way, Björn became helplessly lost in a dense fog. It was so dark that he could not see his hand in front of his face. Instead of worrying about where he was, Björn sat down under a large rock and began to play his fiddle. Suddenly, he heard fairy voices from inside the rock. They were so beautiful that Björn wrote down the words and composed a tune for them on his fiddle.

The verses went like this:

My body is a boat
That lies abandoned on a beach
Without shelter.
Wildly thunder the waves on the shore.
At daybreak sings my heart's despair.

My body is a bird
That huddles against the storm
Without feathers.
No song on the water, no joy evermore.
At daybreak sings my heart's despair.

My body is a harp
That lies forgotten against the wall
Without tune.
Blackened with soot in a maiden's door.
At daybreak sings my heart's despair.

When the fog disappeared, Björn resumed his journey and arrived safely at his uncle's house. Hálfdán warmly greeted him. Then he read the message from the boy's mother, and immediately chastised Björn for drifting around the countryside like a beggar. Using all his powers of persuasion, he soon convinced the lad to find a more acceptable occupation.

Hálfdán loved to play tricks on people. One day he decided to amuse himself by testing Björn's courage. He knew the boy was determined and brave, but he wanted to find out what it would take to shake the boy's confidence. He cast a few spells, created a few illusions, and watched to see what would happen.

That evening, Hálfdán sent Björn to fetch some fishing tackle. The boy found the tackle scattered across the boathouse floor, and playing with the pieces were a dozen or more devils and ghosts. They were screaming, belching flames, vomiting their guts out, and whipping their heads around in circles on their necks.

Björn watched the devils for a while and then calmly, but with considerable difficulty, gathered up the tackle. All the way back to the farmhouse, the devils and ghosts pursued him but Björn pretended not to notice.

When he reached the house, Hálfdán asked what had taken him so long. Björn replied that the tackle was spread across the floor like horse droppings across a field and he had to pick up every piece. With an interested look on his face, Hálfdán asked if he noticed any strange lads playing in the area. Björn said that he had, and that he found them very entertaining.

Another time Hálfdán sent Björn out into a field to watch some lambs. At dusk, twelve men rode by and asked Björn if he wanted to play. Björn agreed, but was a bit surprised by their choice of games. First the men shook their bodies and hopped up and down. Then they popped off their heads and started hitting each other with them. Björn found it painful to watch and even more painful to get hit by one. Not to be outdone, he took off his own head and joined in the competition. They played for quite some time and when they were finished, the men retrieved their own heads, set them backward on their necks and vanished.

Björn also put his head on backward. With great difficulty—he could now only see what was behind him—he moved the flock back to the farm. Hálfdán watched his nephew's progress and when he arrived at the gate, warmly greeted him and asked how his day went.

"Well enough," said Björn. "But for some strange reason, I see things behind me better that those in front of me. I hope I will eventually get used to it."

With a grin, Hálfdán passed a hand over the boy and returned his head to its rightful position.

A few days later, the body of an old woman was

brought to Hálfdán's church for burial. Since it was late in the day and the mourners needed a place to stay, Hálfdán invited them to his house. He asked Björn to fetch extra bedding from the loft of the church.

As Björn descended the ladder with the bedding in his arms, the corpse of the old woman rose up and leaped onto his back. She hooked her legs around his waist and fastened her fingers around his neck, almost choking him to death. "Is this for real?" Björn thought. He walked to the doorway and slammed the corpse against the doorframe. Again and again he tried to remove her but she clung tightly to his back.

Bjön carried the corpse out of the church and all the way to the farmhouse. With this strange burden on his back, he passed Hálfdán, who was on his way to the barn. Hálfdán asked him if everything was all right and Björn replied, "Just fine. But for some reason I'm having trouble fitting through doorways."

Hálfdán laughed at the boy's good humor and released him from his burden. He promised to stop playing tricks and Björn knew that he had finally won his uncle's respect.

A man named Grímur lived near Hálfdán and Björn. One evening his pretty sweet-natured daughter went out with the washing and met a stranger. The man tried to entice her to make love to him but the girl, Valdís, resisted all his sweet-talking. For a short time, the two bantered back and forth, but when Valdís's father found them, he ordered the man to leave his farm. From that day on, the girl could not speak and acted as if she had lost her mind.

Grímur tried everything possible to cure his daughter but nothing worked. In the end, he rode to Hálfdán's house and begged for help. Hálfdán was reluctant to get involved with the girl. He told Grímur that his daughter was under a spell. Someone would have to discover who had cast it and then persuade that person to remove it. What Hálfdán did not tell Grímur was that a rock giant had cast the spell and that it was beyond his power to force the giant to reverse it.

Grímur continued to plead for his daughter's sanity and eventually Hálfdán agreed to help. He warned Grímur that removing a spell was not an easy task. He could only try, but did not promise that he would get the desired results.

Hálfdán summoned all the elves, dwarves, ghosts, and trolls between the Blanda and Öxará rivers but he still worried that even together they might not have enough power. Then he called Björn and asked him if he was brave enough to ride a magical horse across the sea. Since he had never been frightened of a horse before, Björn saw no reason why riding a magical one should be any different.

Hálfdán brought out a bay horse with a dark stripe along its back. He told Björn to ride to the island of Grímsey, find a pinnacle rock, and strike it while saying, "Bergfinnur! Hálfdán summons you out of the rock. He orders you and your wife to meet him at Fell."

Björn rode the horse across the sea, skimming so close to the surface of the water that his feet got soaking wet. He carried out Hálfdán's orders and arrived safely back at the farmhouse. When he dismounted the horse, Björn was surprised to discover that the animal was actually the hip bone of a man. Hálfdán watched him inspect the bone and asked if he like his horse. Björn replied that it was a unique animal and obviously not well fed.

Bergfinnur the troll and his wife arrived at Fell at the appointed hour. Unwilling to admit that he had cast the spell on Valdís, the troll decided to kill the wizard instead. He and his wife hurled rocks down on the elves, dwarves, ghosts, and other trolls, but specifically aimed for Hálfdán. They were so ferocious that Hálfdán had trouble defending himself. Luckily, his sister Hildigunnur heard about the trolls and decided to join in the battle. Together, they forced the troll to admit to casting the spell. Hálfdán commanded the troll to lift the spell and Valdís was immediately cured.

In the end, Björn married Valdís and they lived in prosperity on a farm by the Brædraá River. Björn joyfully played his fiddle well into old age and became a man of wealth who was respected by all.

As for Hálfdán, he too lived a long and prosperous life. When he died, he was warmly greeted in heaven.

Based on Boucher I, 29–33

The Magicians of the Westmann Islands

As the Black Death swept through Iceland, eighteen magicians banded together and sailed to the Westmann Islands. Their plan was to stay alive for as long as possible. After a time, with the use of magic, they watched the plague disappear from the mainland. Afraid to venture back over as a group but curious to know how many people had survived, they decided to send one man on a mission to find out. For this possibly life-threatening task, they chose a magician who was neither the least skilled nor the most skilled among them.

Early in the Easter season, the chosen magician set off for the shores of Iceland with orders to return by Christmas Day. If he did not return, the others would summon a spirit from the dead and send it out to kill him.

The magician safely arrived on the mainland. He travelled back and forth across the countryside and was amazed when he didn't encounter a single living person. Every farm he passed stood quiet and unprotected, all of its inhabitants dead.

One day, he walked up to a farmhouse and discovered that the doors were shut and locked. Hope stirred in his heart that he might finally find someone alive. He knocked on the door and a beautiful young girl ran out and flung her arms around his neck. She greeted him, weeping for joy, because she thought she was the last person alive.

The girl welcomed him into her home and they sat down for a long chat. They discussed everything. She told him what had happened to all the people on her farm and how she had travelled a whole week in every direction and found no one alive. He told her about life in the Westmann Islands and about his travels across the countryside. Then he said that he had to return to his friends by Christmas Day. On hearing this, she begged him to stay with her for as long as possible. Moved by her predicament and perhaps her beauty, he agreed.

Time slipped by and the Christmas season drew near. The magician tried several times to leave, but the girl kept persuading him to postpone his trip. She convinced him that his friends would not be so heartless as to punish him for helping a girl who was all alone in the world. So time after time, the man allowed himself to be convinced to stay.

On Christmas Eve, the magician decided to leave, no matter how persuasively the girl pleaded. When she realized that her words were falling on deaf ears, she made one last desperate attempt to delay him and said, "You will never reach the island by morning. Maybe it is better to die here with me than alone somewhere in the wilderness."

The man recognized the truth in her words. Since there wasn't enough time to reach the island, he decided to stay with the girl and wait for death.

All Christmas morning, the magician sat in gloomy silence. After several attempts to cheer him, the girl asked if he could use his magic and see what the others on the island were doing. He said that he had already looked and they were preparing a spirit. It would arrive on shore later that night.

As the day progressed, the magician became more and more sleepy. He crawled into bed and when the girl sat down beside him, he told her that his drowsiness was probably the beginning of the spirit's attack. Every time he started to fall asleep, the girl shook him awake, demanding that he watch the spirit as it moved across the land and tell her its position. The closer the spirit came, the harder it was for the magician to stay awake. Finally, when the spirit was at the edge of her land, he fell into such a deep sleep that she could not wake him.

A russet-colored vapor entered the farmhouse and gently glided across the room. It took on the shape of a man and drifted toward the girl and the sleeping wizard. The girl watched it approach and asked, "What are you doing here?"

"I am on a mission to kill a magician," the spirit replied. "Please get off the bed. I can not reach him with you in my way."

The girl refused, telling the spirit that if he wanted her to move, he would have to do something for her. The spirit agreed, and she said that she wanted to see how large he could grow. Immediately, he ballooned up and filled the entire house.

"Now I want to see if you can grow very small," said the girl.

The spirit started to shrink and turned himself into a tiny fly, hoping to slip under the girl's arm and attack the magician. But since he was a fly, he couldn't resist landing on a tasty bone that the girl had lying in her lap. He crawled into the marrow hole and was immediately trapped when she shoved a plug into each end.

The girl put the bone in her pocket and woke the magician. He was amazed to discover that he was still alive. He searched everywhere for the spirit and was delighted to tell the girl that it was nowhere in sight. She laughed and said that maybe the magicians of the Westmann Islands were not as strong as he thought. With delight, the wizard agreed and they happily celebrated the rest of Christmas night.

Unfortunately as the New Year approached, the magician grew more and more somber. The girl noticed and asked him what was wrong. He told her that the others were preparing another spirit. They were filling it with all their combined power and sending it to kill him on New Year's Eve. This time, nothing could save him.

On New Year's Eve, the magician watched as the spirit came ashore with great power and great speed. The girl grabbed his hand and ran outside. She led him to a thicket and pushed aside the branches. Underneath was a slab of rock that she lifted to reveal a hidden chamber. They climbed down the dark and gloomy hole, which was dimly lit by a lamp that was made from a human skull and burned only human belly fat. The magician was quite impressed by the ghastly chamber.

In a bed near the lamp lay a ghostly old man with frighteningly blood-red eyes. He addressed the girl, saying, "Something awful must have happened, my child, if have come to me. It has been a long time since last I saw you. What can I do for you?"

The girl told him everything: what had happened to her, what had happened to the wizard, and all she knew about the spirit. When she was finished, the old man asked to see the leg bone with the captured fly inside. He turned it over and over, stroking it.

"Quickly, you must help us!" she cried. "Look! The magician is sleepy. It is a sign that the other spirit is getting closer."

The old man pulled the plug out of the bone and the fly walked out. Stroking and patting the insect, he said, "Off you go—meet the other spirit from the Westmann Islands and swallow it whole."

The fly took off and the moment it was out of the chamber, it began to grow. There was a loud boom as it sailed into the air. In minutes, it grew so large that its upper jaw touched the sky and its lower jaw scraped the ground. It enveloped the spirit sent from the island and saved the magician's life.

The girl and the magician left the underground chamber and returned home. They settled on her farm, got married, and their many children populated the land.

Based on Jón Árnason I, 308–310

SIX

Monsters, Money, and Fairy Tales

Skuggabaldur and Skoffín

A skuggabaldur is the offspring of a female fox and a male cat. They are vicious animals that attack and kill sheep. Whenever a shepherd tries to shoot a skuggabaldur, his gun always misfires and the animal easily escapes.

A skoffín, on the other hand, is the offspring of a male fox and a female cat. They are always killed before they reach adulthood, so they pose little problem for the shepherds.

One time in Húnavatn, flocks of sheep were being stalked and killed by a particularly mean skuggabaldur. In desperation, a crowd of people chased it into a hole near the Blandá River. They began beating the animal and in the moments before the final death blow, it raised its head and said, "Tell the Bollastadir cat that today Skuggabaldur died in this gulley."

The skuggabaldur took one last breath and died. Many in the crowd wondered what the animal meant when it spoke those final words.

One evening, the man who landed the final blow that killed the skuggabaldur passed through Bollastadir and decided to stay the night. During the evening meal, while reclining in the warm living room, he told his story.

An old tomcat was sitting on a beam above the man's head, listening. When the man repeated the skuggabaldur's final words, the cat leaped down and fastened his claws around the man's neck. Its grasp was so tight that within seconds the storyteller was dead.

Based on Jón Árnason I, 610

Naddi

In ancient times, a main road ran from Njardvík to Borgarfjördur, passing over a very steep mountain and running down toward the sea. The road eventually became impassable when a monster, who looked like a man on top and an animal below, decided to live along this road.

Each night, the monster would hide in a rocky canyon on the sea side of the mountain nearest Njardvík, attacking and killing unwary travellers. In the autumn and winter, the people of Njardvík often heard it mumble and thrash among the rocks. They named their monster Naddi or "the mumbler."

One autumn day, Jón Bjarnason was travelling to Njardvík and stopped to rest at a farmhouse. At dusk, he decided to continue his journey. When the farmer and his household heard about Jón's decision, they begged him to wait until morning. The farmer warned him that to reach Njardvík, he would have to pass through the canyon where Naddi lived. It was too risky to confront such an angry monster in the dark.

Determined to travel further that evening, Jón ignored their pleas, and reassured them that he was not in any danger. After thanking them for their hospitality, he continued on the road to Njardvík.

When Jón entered the canyon, Naddi sneaked up behind him and attacked. The two fought hard, rolling over and over, down the side of the mountain.

Their battle brought them all the way to Krossjadar. When they crossed the boundary into that territory, Naddi leaped away from Jón and threw his battle-scarred body into the sea.

Jón arrived at Njardvík, bruised and battered from his fight with Naddi. He spent a month in bed recovering.

Although the Naddi was never seen again, everyone agreed that since he originally came from the sea, it was natural for him to retreat home once he was beaten.

Based on Jón Árnason I, 134–135

Búkolla

This story begins on the day that Búkolla gave birth to a calf. Búkolla was the only cow of a poor old couple, and consequently she was smothered with love and affection.

When the old woman discovered that her cow was pregnant, she was delighted. After many months of anxious waiting, Búkolla went into labor and safely delivered a beautiful calf. Once the birth was over, the old woman ran into the cottage to announce the happy news. But when she returned later in the day to check on the newborn calf, she was horrified to discover that Búkolla was gone.

The old couple searched everywhere—far and near—but they could not find Búkolla. Upset and angry at the loss, they returned home and entered their cottage. Seeing their only son sitting by the fire, the old woman ordered him to leave the house and return only if he found the cow. She handed him some food and a new pair of shoes, and ushered him out the door.

The boy searched for hours until, exhausted and hungry, he stopped to eat a meal. When he was finished, he cried out in desperation, "Moo for me, my Búkolla! If you are alive to hear, moo!"

From far in the distance, he heard the gentle lowing of a cow.

Encouraged by the sound, the boy jumped to his feet and continued to search in the direction of the

sound. On and on he walked until once again fatigue
forced him to stop and eat. When he finished eating,
he shouted, "Moo for me, my Búkolla! If you are alive
to hear, moo!"

To the boy's surprise, he heard a long, low mooing
that sounded much closer than the time before. He
sprang to his feet. Following what he now knew was
Búkolla's call, he reached the edge of a very high cliff.
Sitting with his feet dangling over the ledge, he
shouted again, "Moo for me, my Búkolla! If you are
alive to hear, moo!" The answering cry from Búkolla
came from directly below his feet.

The boy climbed down the side of the cliff and at the
bottom found the entrance to a gigantic cave.
Continuing to follow Búkolla's calls, he ventured deeper
into the cavern. When he found her, he untied her rope
and led her out of the cave and up the side of the cliff.

They travelled for some time before the boy
looked back and realized that a giant she-troll was
pursuing them. The troll was marching along,
dragging a smaller troll behind her. Within seconds,
the boy realized that the troll's strides were so long that
she was gaining on them. Frightened, he turned to the
cow and said, "Búkolla, what should I do?"

To his amazement, she replied, "Take a strand of
hair from my tail and put it on the ground." The boy
immediately obeyed her.

Búkolla gazed down at the hair and murmured:

This hair I lay, and to this hair I say,
Be a mighty flood, I pray,
So only birds may fly this way!

After the cow had spoken these words, the hair
immediately turned into a wide, fast-flowing river.

When the she-troll reached the water's edge, she called out, "A river cannot save you, my boy!" And she turned to the smaller troll she said, "Quickly! Run home and fetch my father's bull."

The small troll ran back to the cave and soon returned with an enormous bull. The bull leaned down and began to drink from the river. He sucked up the water until every last drop was gone.

The boy watched the bull in amazement, knowing that within moments the she-troll would catch up to them again. He turned to the cow and said, "What should we do now, Búkolla?"

Búkolla said, "Take another hair from my tail and lay it on the ground."

The boy did as she asked and the cow said to the hair:

This hair I lay, and to this hair I say,
Be a fierce fire, I pray,
So only birds may fly this way!

And immediately the hair turned into a raging inferno.

When the she-troll reached the flames, she called out, "A fire cannot save you, my boy!" And she turned to the small troll and said, "Bring my father's bull to me."

The small troll brought the bull again and the she-troll led it nearer to the fire. The bull urinated onto the flames, releasing all the water it had drunk from the river. The fire became a pile of dying embers.

The boy and the cow watched the bull pee and knew that the trolls would soon catch up with them. "Búkolla, What should we do now?" the boy asked.

"Take a hair from my tail," the cow replied, "And lay it on the ground." Then she dropped her head toward the hair and said:

This hair I lay, and to this hair I say,
Be a steep mountain, I pray,
So only birds may fly this way!

Immediately the hair turned into a mountain so high that the boy could see nothing but blue sky above it.

When the she-troll arrived at the mountain, she cried out, "A mountain cannot save you, my boy!" Then she turned to the small troll and said, "Quickly! Run home and fetch my father's drill."

The small troll ran back to the cave and soon returned with the drill. The she-troll grabbed it and began drilling a hole straight through the mountain. Luckily for Búkolla and the boy, she grew impatient. As soon as daylight appeared in the hole, she tried to squeeze through it. But the hole was too narrow and her body lodged tightly inside. The harder she tried to escape, the tighter her body stuck. Eventually, she gave up and turned into a huge stone that even today travellers can see poking out of the mountainside.

Búkolla and the boy returned to the cottage and the old couple was overjoyed to see them.

Based on Jón Árnason II, 445–446

The Dreamer and the Money Chest

Once upon a time on a warm Sunday morning, a large group of men pitched their tents on the edge of a beautiful green meadow. Exhausted from their long night's journey, they tethered the horses, crawled into their beds and were soon sound asleep.

One of the men, lying near the doorway of a tent, could not fall asleep. In spite of his fatigue, he lay wide awake, jealously watching the peaceful slumber of the others. Suddenly, a small cloud of pale blue mist appeared out of nowhere. It hovered over the head of a traveller who was sleeping on the far side of the tent. Rubbing his eyes to make sure he was really awake, the man sat up and watched the cloud float over all of the sleeping men and out the door. Amazed by the sight, he wondered what it was and where it was going. He quietly crawled out of bed and followed the blue mist.

Immediately, the man was greeted with blinding sunshine. Blinking his eyes while trying to focus, he searched for the mist and saw it floating slowly across the meadow. He followed the cloud until it stopped, hovering over the bleached skull of a horse that lay partially hidden in the grass. Buzzing in and out of the skull was a swarm of noisy blue flies. The mist enveloped the flies and together they entered the skull.

A short time later, the cloud floated out alone and began to travel further across the meadow. It stopped at the edge of a trickling brook. Restlessly, it moved up and down the water's edge, as though frantically searching for a way to cross. Curious, the man placed his whip across the tiny stream and the mist happily floated along it and over the water.

The mist continued across the meadow until it came to a small hill and then disappeared into the ground. The man patiently waited for it to reappear and a short time later, it did.

The cloud drifted back through the meadow and over the brook, again using the man's whip for a bridge. It reentered the tent, and as the man watched, it hovered over the same sleeping traveller and then disappeared from sight. Confused by what he had seen, but now extremely tired, the man crawled into his bed and fell asleep.

The sun was just beginning to set when the group of travellers woke up, took down their tents, and prepared for their nighttime journey. As they packed and loaded the horses, the men talked about their lives, families, and past expeditions. But mostly they talked about money.

"I sure wish the dream I had today was real," said the traveller who had slept under the mist.

"What was your dream?" asked the man who had followed it across the meadow. "What did you see?"

The dreamer said, "I crawled out of the tent and began to walk across the meadow. Suddenly, I was standing before a beautiful building. There was a crowd of people milling around outside and as soon as I arrived, we entered the most magnificent hall. A party was in full swing and I joined in the fun, singing, dancing, and having a wonderful time.

"I enjoyed the party for a while, and then decided to leave. As I stepped outside, a vast expanse of green grass lay before me. I walked for a long time until I reached the bank of a very wide and turbulent river. I desperately wanted to cross it, but no matter how hard I tried, I could not find a bridge.

"As I walked up and down the bank, a huge giant came striding toward me. In his hand he carried the trunk of a very large tree. He laid it across the river and I easily crossed to the other side.

"Again I walked for a very long time, until I came to a hill with an opening in the side of it. Thinking that I might find a buried treasure, I went inside, but all I found was one chest. The chest was full of gold but so heavy I couldn't lift it. I counted the coins for hours, and only touched a portion of what was in that chest. Eventually, I just gave up and returned to the tent."

This story pleased the man who had followed the mist. He laughed and said, "Come my friend, let's fetch that money. If one person cannot count it all, surely two of us can."

"Fetch the money!" the dreamer said. "Are you mad? It was only a dream. How would we know where to find it?"

Seeing the determination on the other man's face, the dreamer decided to follow him across the meadow. The two men walked along the same path that the mist had travelled. First they arrived at the horse skull and the man said, "Here is the magnificent hall where the party took place."

They went a bit further and stopped at the tiny brook. The man said, "Here is your wide and turbulent river." And showing the dreamer his whip he said, "I am the giant and this is the tree trunk that was used as a bridge."

The dreamer was amazed by this story. When they

arrived at the hill, the two men began to dig into the ground and soon uncovered a chest filled with pieces of gold.

Together, they carried the heavy chest all the way back to their campsite. Along the way, the man told the dreamer all about following the mist, and that when he heard about the dream, he knew exactly where to find the hidden gold.

Based on Jón Árnason I, 342–343

The Ghost and His Buried Treasure

In the north of Iceland there lived a penny-pinching farmer. He hoarded all his money, and even his kind and charitable wife could not temper his voracious greed. Everyone in the region knew of this man and many believed that he was extremely wealthy.

One winter the farmer fell ill and died. The men in the community helped to bury him, but when the time came to settle his estate, they realized that no one could find his money. They asked his widow if she knew where it was, but she told them that she didn't have a single shilling. Since she was an honest woman, they believed what she told them, and guessed that the old farmer had buried the money in a place where he hoped no one would find it.

Winter passed and the people in the area started noticing that they had a new ghost. They all believed that it was the dead farmer, wandering the earth trying to protect his hidden treasure. The ghost's hauntings became so disruptive that most of the workers on the widow's farm threatened to leave the following spring if it didn't stop. Without workers, the widow would be forced to abandon her home and sell the property.

One day, a man came to the widow asking for a job. Desperate for the help, she immediately hired him. Soon after he had arrived, he too started noticing the frightening antics of the ghost. Curious to know if the rumors about the farmer were true, he asked his mistress if her late husband had possessed a large amount of money. But just like before, she said that she knew nothing about it. If he had hoarded any money and buried it on the property, the secret had died with him.

When market day arrived, the hired man bought, among other things, a sheet of iron and a length of white linen. He returned to the farm, and using his skills as a blacksmith, formed the iron into a breast plate and gloves. Then he sewed the linen into a flowing white shroud.

Time passed and once again the days grew short and the nights long and dark. One evening, when everyone was asleep, the hired man tied the breastplate around his chest, pulled on the gloves and threw the linen shroud over his entire body. He went into the churchyard and walked back and forth over the farmer's grave, tossing a piece of silver in the air and catching it in the palm of his hand.

Suddenly, a ghost rose up from the grave and stood before the man. The ghost asked, "Are you one of us?"

"Yes," said the man.

"Then let me touch you," said the ghost, and he reached for the man.

The hired man offered the ghost an iron clad hand. The ghost, after feeling how cold it was, said, "You must be a ghost, but why are you walking the earth?"

"So I can enjoy my silver piece," said the man, showing him the shiny coin lying in the palm of his hand.

Satisfied with that answer, the ghost turned away. He climbed over the churchyard wall and the hired man followed him. When they reached the edge of the field, the ghost opened up a hole in a small hill and pulled out a money chest.

All night long, the ghost and the man played with the coins. But just before dawn, the ghost started putting them back into the chest. The man asked if he could take one last look at the money and the ghost agreed. He peeked into the chest, grabbed a handful of coins, and scattered them across the grass.

"I am not so sure you are a ghost," said the indignant ghost.

"Yes I am," said the man. "Touch me again." And he offered the ghost his other hand.

The ghost touched it and reluctantly said, "I guess you are."

The ghost started collecting the scattered coins, and became angry when the man threw them into the grass again. Turning toward him, the frustrated ghost said that only a living person would throw around coins. He must be lying. He was really alive and was planning to cheat him out of his money.

The man denied the ghost's accusations and was surprised when, suddenly, the ghost grabbed him by the chest. Feeling only the coldness of the iron plate, the ghost let go of him and said, "What you say must be true. You are as cold as I am."

Once again, the ghost collected the coins. This time, the man was too afraid to antagonize him any further and allowed him to finish the job. When all the money was safely stashed in the chest, the hired man said, "Let me put my silver piece in with your money."

The ghost agreed and tucked the silver coin into his chest. Together they set the chest into the hole. Then the ghost covered it over with dirt and grass so that no one could tell that the ground had ever been disturbed.

The ghost and the hired man returned to the churchyard and the ghost asked, "Where is your grave?"

"On the other side of the church," said the hired man.

"You go into your grave first," said the ghost.

"No," said the man. "You go first."

They continued to bicker back and forth until the sun peeked over the eastern horizon, forcing the ghost to jump into his grave.

The hired man returned to the farmhouse, found a large barrel, and filled it with water. Then he threw in his shroud and the metal breastplate and gloves, knowing that the water would prevent the ghost from smelling the earth on them. When he was finished, he returned to the hill, dug up the chest of coins, and submerged it in the water too.

That night after everyone was in bed, the ghost arrived, sniffing and snuffing all around the house, searching for his lost gold. The hired man, lying near the door, heard the ghost strike a mighty blow on the side of the barrel, but he never found his treasure.

Frustrated, the ghost left the farmhouse. The hired man followed him out the door, and by using a bit of magic, he sent the ghost back into his grave and no one was bothered by him again. All the hauntings stopped and the lucky hired man married the farmer's widow. They lived together for many years, happily spending the ghost's hidden treasure.

Based on Jón Árnason I, 258–259

Black Cloak Hill

In ancient times a woman named Blákápa, or Black Cloak, owned much of the land in the Fljót district. She was a domineering woman and hated it when the people who lived further up the valley trespassed on her land. Finally, in an attempt to keep them out, she built a huge stone wall all the way across the valley, from cliff face to cliff face.

In accordance with her funeral instructions, Blákápa and all her possessions were buried in a large hill at one end of the wall. She said that anyone who could walk backward along the entire length of the wall without stopping or looking behind could claim her treasure.

Many have tried to walk the wall, but no one has succeeded. One time, several men decided to search for the treasure without attempting to walk the wall. They started digging into the hill, and suddenly, the entire valley below them appeared to be on fire! Frightened, they stopped digging and the fire disappeared.

Today, there are few visible signs of Blákápa's wall. But, since no one has claimed her treasure, it probably still lies buried deep inside Black Cloak Hill.

Based on Jón Árnason III, 118–119

The Story of Jón Ásmundarson

Young Jón Ásmundarson was born in the Borgarfjördur district, the oldest son in a very poor family. One year, when the crops were especially poor, his father was forced to abandon their farm and scatter his children across the country, leaving them to be raised in other families.

Jón was taken to Reykjavík, to the home of a priest named Kristján. Kristján loved the boy and raised him as his only son. Jón grew into a handsome, hard-working young man and before long, had a reputation for being the strongest youth in the region. Quiet by nature, Jón seldom spoke to anyone, but his helpful spirit made him a favorite in the priest's household.

One summer, a trading ship arrived in Reykjavík harbor. It was owned by a prosperous foreign merchant and was just one vessel in a large and thriving shipping business. Kristján, along with many of the other men from Reykjavík, annually traded with this merchant.

One day, while conducting business on board the ship, Kristján overheard several crew members arguing about which man was the strongest. To settle their debate, the muscular merchant walked across the ship's deck to where four barrels of rye lay bound together by a sturdy rope. He seized the rope in his hands and lifted the barrels up to his knees. After setting them back down, he announced to his men, "If any man can lift more than me, I will reward him with three half-pounds of gold."

Kristján finished his trading and hurried home. He found his foster son Jón and told him about the weight-lifting merchant, his challenge to the crew, and the promise of gold. He knew that Jón was very strong and was sure to win the prize. Jón agreed to the challenge and the two men returned to the vessel.

Once on board, Kristján announced that his foster son wanted to test his strength. The merchant motioned toward the barrels and watched to see what the boy could do. To his amazement, Jón lifted all four barrels onto his shoulders and, acting as though they were as light as a bundle of feathers, carried them back and forth across the deck.

When the merchant realized that he had to make good on his bet, his face flushed with anger, but he willingly counted out the gold and handed it to Jón. As they were about to leave, he invited Jón to come back and visit him before the ship set sail at the end of summer. Jón accepted the invitation and he and Kristján happily returned home with the gold.

Later that summer, shortly before the merchant's ship was scheduled to leave the harbor, the priest reminded Jón of his invitation. The two men boarded the trading ship and were warmly greeted by the merchant. He suggested that they talk in his cabin and when they reached the ladder that extended below the deck, he turned to Kristján and said, "My friend, please stay on deck. I would like to have a private conversation with this young man."

Kristján refused to stay behind. Once they were inside the cabin, the merchant said to Jón, "I have another challenge for you. At this same time next year, I will return to Iceland and bring a young lad for you to wrestle. If you win, I will reward you with five pounds of gold."

Jón agreed to the match and then he and the priest returned to shore and the merchant sailed out of the harbor.

One afternoon, while winter still enveloped the land, Kristján reminded Jón of the foreign merchant's challenge. Jón asked his father why he was worried about such an easy match.

"This match will not be easy," Kristján said. "The merchant lied to us. The lad he spoke of will actually be a wicked and massive man. The man will tear you to pieces unless we think of a way to protect you. We must prepare! When the summer is in its third week, the merchant's ship will return to our harbor."

Still not bothered by Kristján's dire warning, Jón left the room and promptly forgot all about the wrestling match.

Summer arrived and the merchant's ship was spotted making its way toward Reykjavík. As soon as the priest heard the news, he began to prepare Jón to meet his formidable opponent. He dressed his foster son in a black woolen peasant's robe and clasped a belt around his waist. Then he handed Jón a tiny, sharp-edged dagger, telling him to keep it hidden in his hand and his hand tucked in the sleeve of his robe.

Then he told Jón not to resist the man's attacks. "He will fling you over his shoulders," said Kristján. "But I will make sure that you land on your feet. Fight with him for a while and then challenge him to remove his shaggy coat. Say that only by removing it can he truly prove his superior strength. He will take it off and when he attacks you for the second time, thrust the dagger deep into his chest."

Jón and Kristján arrived at the beach. They watched the ship's anchor settle into the water and then, as Kristján had predicted, a gigantic man dressed in a shaggy coat jumped into a boat and rowed toward shore. The moment the boat touched the beach, the giant man jumped out, rushed at Jón, and seized him by the arms. He lifted the boy above his head and threw him into the air. Jón sailed high into the sky but landed firmly on his feet. After several throws and several safe landings, Jón decided that it was time to make the challenge.

He called out to the man, taunting him and saying that to truly prove his superior strength he must remove his coat. As the man flung the shaggy coat aside, Jón cautiously slipped the sharp dagger into his right hand and prepared for another attack. He knew that this huge man was so strong that he should have been killed. Instead, with the help of magic, his black robe was protecting him from the powerful blows.

Blinded by rage, the man raced toward Jón, expecting to kill him with one final blow. He screamed in disbelief when the tiny dagger plunged deep into his chest. The wrestling match continued, both men bruised and bleeding, but finally ended with Jón killing his opponent.

Kristján and Jón boarded the trading ship, found the merchant and warmly greeted him. Surprised to see that Jón was still alive, the merchant said, "How was the wrestling match?"

"Look toward the shore," Kristján said, "You will see your man lying dead near the water's edge. That, my friend, is how the match went."

The merchant saw the dead man and angrily said, "You are a dishonest man. This boy was protected by magic. He did not win by using his own strength."

"That may be true," said the priest. "But he fought fairly and deserves his reward. You lied when you said that he would be wrestling another boy. You sent an evil giant of a man and still my boy defeated him."

The merchant could not deny Kristján's accusation and reluctantly placed a five pound bag of gold into Jón's hands. Setting his anger aside, he asked Jón to visit him once more before his ship sailed from port at the end of the summer. Jón accepted the invitation and returned home with his father.

A short time before the merchant's ship was scheduled to sail from Reykjavík, the priest reminded Jón of his invitation. After promising to remain with him throughout the entire visit, Kristján escorted Jón aboard the vessel and warmly greeted the merchant.

Again the merchant tried to pull Jón aside and speak privately with him, but a determined Kristján stayed close to his foster son. In frustration, the merchant said, "You do not need to stand so close! What we are talking about is none of your business."

Kristján refused to back away. He said to the merchant, "I will not leave the boy's side. But I promise I will not interrupt your conversation."

Aware of the hovering priest, the merchant said to Jón, "I have a new challenge for you. When I return next summer, I will test your strength against a young dog. If you win the contest, I will reward you with seven and a half pounds of good quality gold."

Jón agreed to the challenge and the three men parted ways, Jón and Kristján returning to shore and the merchant sailing out to sea.

Fall settled over Iceland and then slowly changed to winter. When winter was almost over and Jón had not mentioned the upcoming fight, Kristján asked him if he was prepared for the merchant's arrival.

"No, I'm not," said Jón.

"This fight will be as difficult as the last one," said Kristján. "The merchant has lied to you again. He said that your opponent would be a young dog, but he is bringing a large and vicious deer-hound. The merchant's ship will arrive before a half month of summer has past. You must prepare for this fight! The dog will tear you apart. Your strength is nothing compared to his.

Jón sighed. Then he looked at the priest and said, "Figure something out for me." He left the room and never thought about the fight again.

Summer arrived and before long, a ship appeared on the horizon, sailing toward Reykjavík. Knowing that it was the merchant's vessel, Kristján went to Jón and said, "The merchant's ship is in the harbor. You must prepare to meet your challenger."

The priest dressed his foster son in the same black woolen robe, only this time it was woven through with links of iron. Then he handed Jón a spear and showed him how the barbs on the head could spring apart. Once he stabbed the dog, the barbs would tear the animal's flesh into pieces. Kristján shoved a piece of raw meat on the end of the spear and told Jón to thrust the spear with all his strength down the dog's throat.

They walked to the seashore together. No sooner had the anchor dropped from the merchant's ship than a small boat sped away from it and quickly approached the beach. A large and vicious deer-hound jumped into the water and ran toward Jón. In a mad fury the animal attacked! The dog tried to tear Jón into pieces, but the iron in his robe protected him and saved his life.

Again and again the dog retreated and then rushed back at Jón, each time attacking with greater strength and viciousness. Jón managed to survive each assault and patiently waited for his chance to strike. Keeping the piece of meat dangling under the dog's nose, he waited. Finally, the dog opened his mouth to bite and Jón thrust the spear deep into his throat. Immediately, the animal collapsed, dead at Jón's feet.

After the fight, Jón and Kristján boarded the merchant's ship. "We have come for the gold," Kristján said. "My foster son earned it, fair and square."

The merchant tried to control his anger. His face flushed and his lips swelled. "Fair and square!" he shouted. "He may have fought bravely enough, but he was protected by iron and magic. He has no claim to my gold. He did not keep to our agreement."

"Neither did you," said the priest. "You said that he would fight a young dog but instead you sent a vicious wild beast!"

The merchant could not deny the truth in Kristján's words. He quickly regained his composure and handed Jón the promised seven and a half pounds of gold. Before they left the ship, he invited Jón to visit him once more before he left Iceland at the end of summer. Jón accepted the invitation, and followed by his father, left the ship and returned home.

At the end of summer, when the ship was ready to leave the harbor, Kristján again reminded Jón of his promise to visit the merchant. The ship's anchor was being pulled out of the water as the two men boarded the vessel. Like their two previous visits, the merchant tried to talk to Jón alone in his cabin. This time, they were below deck when the merchant turned on

Kristján and angrily cried out, "Stand back! Stop your meddling. This conversation does not concern you."

"I do not wish to intrude," Kristján politely said. "But I will not leave my boy's side." The priest spoke so firmly that the merchant knew it was useless to argue. He led them into his cabin and pulled down a book from one of his shelves. He opened the front cover and removed a loose page that had been torn from another book. He quickly waved the page in front of Jón's face, hoping to prevent Kristján from seeing what was written on it.

After tucking it back into the book and placing the book on the shelf, the merchant said to Jón, "I have a final challenge for you. When I return next summer, you must bring me the book from which that page of text was torn. If you fail, I will know that you are a spineless fool. If you bring me the book, I will reward you with fifteen pounds of good quality gold."

After agreeing to the challenge, Jón and Kristján returned home and the merchant sailed out to sea.

During the last week of summer, the priest asked Jón if he had given any thought to the merchant's challenge. He was surprised when Jón said that it had never crossed his mind. "Did you recognize anything that was written on the book page that he flapped in front of your face?" asked Kristján.

"No," said Jón. "I couldn't read a single word."

"That doesn't surprise me," said the priest. "The page was torn from the Devil's manual. I must warn you that this task will be very difficult. I know of only one man who can help us. He is my brother and a priest in the world below. You must travel to the underworld and spend the entire winter with him there, from the first day to the last."

Jón packed for the long journey and when he was finished, Kristján handed him a letter of introduction and a ball of thread, which would unravel ahead of him and guide the way. He wished his foster son a safe journey and left him with two warnings. First, he must never, not once, look back toward home. And second, from that moment on, he must not utter a single word for the entire winter.

After promising to heed his warnings, Jón reassured his father that the challenge would be easily accomplished. He said goodbye to all his friends and tossed the ball onto the ground. With one end of the thread held tightly in his hand, he followed the ball as it quickly rolled away.

Later in the day, Jón reached a mountain just north of Reykjavík. The ball rolled into the opening of a cave and down a long, dark and dangerous passageway. Jón struggled to keep up and followed it deep into the belly of the earth. Several times he stopped, trying to decide whether to keep going or turn back. Each time the ball tugged on the thread in his hand, encouraging him to continue.

Jón followed the ball for a long time before finally reaching the end of the passageway. He stepped into the light and was pleased to see a lush green meadow stretching out before him. And far off in the distance, he saw a farm that was as big as an entire town.

The ball started rolling over the grass, and Jón followed it until it came to a stop at the entrance to one of the houses. He picked up the ball and knocked on the door. A few moments later it was opened by the most beautiful girl Jón had ever seen. Without saying a word, he nodded a greeting and handed her his father's letter. She silently took the note and the ball of thread and left Jón standing alone on the stoop.

A few minutes later, she returned. Taking him by the hand, she led him along several hallways and into a small room. It was furnished with a table, a chair, a bench, and a bed.

Day after day, Jón lived alone in that room. He never heard another human voice nor saw another human being, except the girl when she came each day to silently serve his meals and make his bed.

Days and then weeks passed. When Jón thought that the winter must be over, a tall and handsome man, dressed in the long black robes of a priest, entered his room. He knew immediately that it was Kristján's brother.

In a sweet and kind voice, the priest greeted Jón and said, "Do you know how long you have been here?"

Jón remained silent but shook his head back and forth.

"You have done well to keep silent for so long," said the priest. "You can speak now. Winter is over and we are enjoying the first days of summer." Then the priest handed Jón a book and said, "You have completed your task. Here is the book you need. Take good care of it and pass it safely into my brother's hands.

"Tell my brother that the owner of the book will miss it at about the same time as the merchant's ship arrives in your harbor. He must board the vessel the moment it sets anchor and purchase the entire ship's cargo. Tell him to unload all the goods and see them safely on shore before handing that book to the merchant. I must warn you that the Devil will reclaim his book from the very hands of the merchant.

"Hurry and pack your things. You must leave today. The ship will arrive in Reykjavík's harbor at the end of this week. Greet my brother and give him my love. Don't forget to tell him everything that I have told you. My daughter will guide you out of the cavern." And with those final words, the priest left Jón's room.

The priest's daughter sadly led Jón out of his room, away from the farm, and toward the passageway to the outside world. They walked side by side, holding hands. With their forced silence finally broken, they happily chatted about everything and anything until they reached the point where the girl could go no further.

She told Jón how to find his way home and then said, "My heart is breaking at the thought of never seeing you again. I wish we could stay together, but you can not live below and I can not live in the world above."

With tears streaming down her face, she handed Jón the ball of thread and then hugged him close. "I want you to know that in a few months, I will give birth to your child," she said. "If it is a boy, I will send him to you when he reaches the age of six. If it is a girl, I will send her to you when she is twelve. Please treat our child with kindness."

With a grieving heart, Jón threw down the ball and followed it along a smooth and well-lit passageway. The scenery around him was so delightful that he didn't notice when he passed from the world below to the world above.

At the end of the first week of summer, Jón arrived in Reykjavík. After greeting all his friends, he handed Kristján the Devil's manual and passed on all the messages from his brother.

The next day, the merchant's ship arrived in the harbor. As the anchor dropped, Kristján steered his boat alongside and waited to board. He climbed on deck, and with a voice as cold as a northeast wind, greeted the merchant. He offered to buy the merchant's entire cargo, telling him that the past winter had been harsh and provisions scarce throughout the country.

The two men agreed on a price and Kristján ordered that everything be unloaded immediately. When all the supplies were safely on shore, Kristján and Jón re-boarded the vessel. When the merchant saw Jón, he asked if he had succeeded in fulfilling his task. In response, Kristján handed him the book. The merchant was speechless. He stared at the Devil's manual and without saying a word, handed Jón his reward money.

Jón took the gold. Then he bade the merchant farewell and the two men quickly jumped into their rowboat. The moment they stepped on shore, the sea turned rough and stormy. They looked back to where the merchant's ship was anchored and saw that it had vanished. Both men knew that the Devil had reclaimed his book.

Jón returned home and for the next six months succumbed to grief over losing his true love. Kristján noticed the change in his foster son's behavior and accused him of falling in love with a girl from the underworld. When Jón did not respond to the accusation, Kristján offered him one of his own daughters for a wife, hoping that she would free him from his all-consuming sadness.

Jón chose the youngest of the priest's three girls. After they were married, he built a house and started farming the best piece of farmland in the area. The couple had several children and for years, lived in peaceful prosperity. But no matter how hard he tried, Jón never forgot the beautiful girl from the underworld.

Twelve years passed and one day, while sitting in the living room with his family, Jón heard a knock at the door. He sent his six-year-old son to see who was there. The child returned and announced that a beautiful little girl was waiting outside. She had sweetly asked him to say that she wished to speak to her father.

A smile, as bright as a ray of sunshine, spread across Jón's face. He jumped up and ran to the door. The moment the little girl saw him, she fell into his open arms and wrapped hers tightly around his neck. She kissed his face and fondly called him Father.

With joy and love in his heart, Jón listened as the girl passed on a message of love from her mother. Then he took her by the hand, led her into the house, and introduced her to his wife and the other children. Jón had shared the story of his trip to the underworld with his wife and since she loved him very much, she warmly welcomed his child.

Jón named his daughter Sigrídur and she grew into a lovely and accomplished young lady. At the end of three years, Sigrídur asked for her father's permission to visit her mother in the underworld. Jón willingly granted the request and told her that she could stay for a year. He asked her to give her mother his deepest love.

Sigrídur travelled to the underworld and when the year was over, returned to her father. The entire family was delighted when she finally arrived back home. Later in the evening, she took her father aside and gave him her mother's dying farewell and the message that he too would die in one month's time.

The news of his imminent death did not frighten Jón. He spent the next month just like any other month, enjoying his life to the fullest. He settled his estate, leaving a large portion of his property to Sigrídur and all his personal wealth to his wife and other children. When he knew that all his loved ones were well taken care of, Jón died. Many in the community mourned his passing and bitterly wept at the loss of such a good man and a faithful friend.

Years later, Sigrídur married a young and talented peasant. Together they built a prosperous farm and raised a large family. Like her father and stepmother, Sigrídur and her husband lived happy and contented lives, watching their descendants spread throughout the south of Iceland.

Based on Jón Árnason I, 313–319

Bibliography

Note that Icelandic authors are, by Icelandic convention, alphabetized by their given names, rather than their patronymics.

Almqvist, Bo. "Dead Child Legends Westward Bound," in *Viking Ale: Studies on Folklore Contacts between the Northern and the Western Worlds*. Éilís Ní Dhuibhne-Almqvist and Séamas Ó Catháin, eds. Aberystwyth: Boethius Press, 1991: 155–165.

_____. "The dead from the Sea in Old Icelandic Tradition," in *Islanders and Water Dwellers: Proceedings of the Celtic-Nordic-Baltic Folklore Symposium held at University College, Dublin, 16–19 June 1996. Dublin, 2000*. Patricia Lysaght, Séamas Ó Catháin, and Daíthi Ó hÓgáin, eds. 1–18.

_____. "Scandinavian and Celtic Folklore Contacts in the Earldom of Orkney," *Viking Ale* (see above) 1–29.

Boucher, Alan, ed. *The Iceland Traveller: A Hundred Years of Adventure*. Reykjavík: Iceland Review, 1989.

Boucher, Alan, trans. *Ghosts, Witchcraft and the Other World* (Icelandic Folktales I). Reykjavík: Iceland Review, 1977.

_____. *Elves, Trolls and Elemental Beings* (Icelandic Folktales II). Reykjavík: Iceland Review, 1977.

Einar Guðmundsson. *Þjóðsögur og þættir I* (Folktales and Stories) Hafnarfjörður: Skuggsjá, 1981.

Einar Ólafur Sveinsson. *The Folk Stories of Iceland*. Benedikt Benediktz, trans. Anthony Faulkes, ed. and revised by Einar G. Ólafur Pétursson. London: Viking Society, 2003.

Gunnell, Terry. "The Coming of the Christmas Visitors: Folk Legends Concerning the Attacks on Icelandic Farmhouses Made by Spirits at Christmas." *Northern*

Studies: The Journal of the Scottish Society for Northern Studies, 38 (2004). 51–75.

_____. "Mists, Magicians and Murderous Children: International Migratory Legends Concerning the 'Black Death' in Iceland." *Northern Lights: Following Folklore in North Western Europe: Essays in Honour of Bo Almqvist*. Séamas Ó Catháin, ed. Dublin, 2001: 47–59.

_____. "The Return of Sæmundur: Origins and Analogues," in *Þjóðlíf og ýjóðtrú: Ritgerðir helaaðar Jóni Hnefli Aðalsteinssyni*. Reykjavík: Þjóðsaga, 1998: 87–111.

Hallfreður Örn Eiríksson [With Helga Jóhannsdóttir]. *The Recording of Icelandic Folklore*. Reykjavík, 1974.

_____. "Some Icelandic Ghost Fabulates," *Arv* 49 (1993): 117–122.

Jón Árnason, translated by George E. J. Powell and Eiríkur Magnússon. *Icelandic Legends*. Ceredigion: Llanerch, 1995.

Jón Árnason and Magnús Grímsson. *Íslenzk Æfintyri* (Icelandic Fairy Tales). Reykjavík: Einar Þorðarson 1852.

_____. *Íslenzkar Þjóðsögur og ævintýri* (Icelandic Folktales and Fairy Tales), Leipzig: J. C. Hinrich, 1862–1864; republished and updated in six volumes 1954–1961.

Jón Hnefill Aðalsteinsson. "Wrestling with a Ghost in Icelandic Popular Belief." *Arv* 43 (1987) 7–20.

_____. "Folk Narrative and Norse Mythology." *Arv* 46 (1990) 115–122.

_____. "The Testimony of Waking Consciousness and Dreams in Migratory Legends Concerning Human Encounters with the Hidden People." *Arv* 49 (1993) 123–131.

_____. "Sæmundr Fróði: A Medieval Master of Magic." *Arv* 50 (1994) 117–132.

_____. "Six Icelandic Magicians after the Time of Sæmundr Fróði." *Arv* 52 (1996) 49–62.

Jón Þorkelsson. *Þjóðsögur og munnmæli* (Folktales and Oral Accounts). Reykjavík: Bókfells útgáfa, 1956.

Kvideland, Reimund, and Henning K. Sehmsdorf, eds. *Scandinavian Folk Belief and Legend*. Minneapolis: University of Minnesota, 1998.

Maurer, Konrad. *Islandische Volkssagen der Gegenwart* (Icelandic Folk Legends). Leipzig: J. C. Hinrich, 1860.

Reidar Christiansen. *The Migratory Legends: A Proposed List of Types with a Systematic Catalogue of the Norwegian Variants*. Helsinki: Suomalainen tiedeakaternia, 1958.

Sigfús Sigfússon. *Íslenzkar þjóðsögur og sagnir* (Icelandic Folktales and Legends) I–XVI, 1922–1958; republished and updated 1984–1993. Reykjavík: Víkingaútgáfan

Simpson, Jacqueline, trans. and ed. *Icelandic Folktales and Legends*. Berkeley: University of California Press, 1972.

———. *Legends of Icelandic Magicians*. Cambridge: D. S. Brewer and Rowman and Littlefield, 1975.

———. *Scandinavian Folktales*. London: Penguin, 1988.

Viðar Hreinsson, Robert Cook, et al., eds. *The Complete Sagas of Icelanders, I–V*. Reykjavík: Leifur Eríksson Publishers, 1997.

Þórbergur Þórðarson and Sigurður Nordal. *Gráskinna hin meiri* (The Longer Grayskin). Reykjavík: Þjóðsaga, 1962.